You could say the three of us were like puzzle pieces that clicked together after being turned every which way.

You know they fit, but it takes you a few tries before they snap into place.

KEEPING IT REAL

BY PAULA CHASE

 GREENWILLOW BOOKS

AN IMPRINT OF HarperCollinsPublishers

Keeping It Real. Copyright © 2021 by Paula Chase

The text of this book is set in Joanna MT.
Book design by Sylvie Le Floc'h

Library of Congress
Cataloging-in-Publication Data

Names: Chase, Paula, author.
Title: Keeping it real / Paula Chase.
Description: First edition. | New York : Greenwillow Books, an Imprint of HarperCollins Publishers, [2021] |
Audience: Ages 8–12. | Audience: Grades 4–6. | Summary: Fourteen-year-old Marigold's family owns Flexx Unlimited,
a hip-hop lifestyle company, and she attends the elite school Flowered Arms Academy, but she has never felt entirely
comfortable in the mostly White school, and she prefers to hang out with Justice, relatively new to the school, but a star
basketball player; so enrolling in Style High with him, a trainee program funded by Mari's family, seems like a good way
to spend the summer—until she meets Kara, who obviously hates Mari and seems determined to turn Justice against her.
Identifiers: LCCN 2021036676 (print) | LCCN 2021036677 (ebook) | 9780062965707 (paperback) |
ISBN 9780062965714 (epub)
Subjects: LCSH: African American girls—Juvenile fiction. | African American families—Juvenile fiction. | Apprenticeship
programs—Juvenile fiction. | Fathers and daughters—Juvenile fiction. | Secrecy—Juvenile fiction. | Sisters—Juvenile
fiction. | Friendship—Juvenile fiction. | Young adult fiction. | CYAC: African Americans—Fiction. | Apprentices—
Fiction. | Fathers and daughters—Fiction. | Secrets—Fiction. | Sisters—Fiction. | Friendship—Fiction.
Classification: LCC PZ7.C38747 Ke 2021 (print) | LCC PZ7.C38747 (ebook) | DDC 813.6 [Fic]—dc23
LC record available at https://lccn.loc.gov/2021036676   LC ebook record available at https://lccn.loc.gov/2021036677

22 23 24 25 26 PC/CWR 10 9 8 7 6 5 4 3 2 1   First Greenwillow paperback edition, 2022
Greenwillow Books

To any and every one of us who heard that we were "acting white." Our Black is just as beautiful.

PROLOGUE

Kara came in hating me.

I was an uppity Hill girl, to her.

And she was just another charity case my parents loved to take on to prove they were still Pea Head and Nut from around the way.

We could have gone on forever never meeting if it weren't for Justice.

CHAPTER .1.

"**A**re you going to say happy friendversary or what?" I bugged my eyes out at my phone. Justice's shoulders, broad and toned from the basketball team's mandatory morning workouts, took up most of the screen. That and his tank top, bright white like he'd just taken it out of the package, against the dark wood of his bed's headboard.

"You working real hard to get me with this friendversary stuff, huh?"

He was laid back, headphones on so his mother wouldn't hear me talking if she burst into his bedroom, something she did whenever he was on the phone. First it was annoying, then I realized why she did it.

We were only in the eighth grade—for one more day

at least—but Jus was already getting sniffs from colleges to play ball. One time, Ms. Lisa came in the room and went off. "I mean it, Justice. Don't let one of these little White girls get you thinking their daddy be fine with you calling them just 'cause you winning games for Flowereds."

I could tell he'd heard the conversation a million times because he cut his eyes my way but then kept it respectful with, "Ma. It's Marigold. You can stop tripping, thanks."

Then, like she hadn't just thrown much shade, she came over—head peeking into the camera—and waved. "How you doing, Mari? How's your mom?"

I liked Ms. Lisa. She was OG real. And that explained why Justice had no chill. He'd say stuff off the rip like just because it was the truth it couldn't hurt people's feelings. I always acted like I was good with whatever real gems he dropped. If I didn't, he'd say I was bougie or worse, that I was being Flo—his way of saying I was acting like the rich, White kids at our private school, Flowered Arms.

Bougie barely bothered me. Mainly because I was.

I was not Flo, though.

Right on cue, Justice said, "Friendversary must be a Flo thing. I can't fade it."

"You're literally the Flowered Arms poster boy, Mr. Ball

So Hard," I said, calling him by the name the posters all around our school called him. Had him flexin' shooting a three-pointer. Basketball season had ended months ago, but the posters were still there. At least the ones that hadn't been taken by students who had gotten Justice to autograph them.

I'd been going to Flo-A since second grade. Justice had only been there since sixth and still some people knew his name and not mine. Did I mention I'm the only Black girl in our grade? Now who more Flo?

I refused to let him off easy. "You repping whether you like it or not. But whatever. Friendversaries are real. And today is two years to the day that you realized being down with me was where it's at. So, give me my cred."

I gave him two snaps—snapping my fingers and raising my eyebrow at him.

"Your confidence got me shook. You always get your way, huh?" he asked.

I joked it off. "I don't always get my way, but I really like to."

His thumb smoothed down the hair on his eyebrow. It was something he did when he was thinking.

"Yeah, I guess you probably do," he said. His shoulder jerked and a small explosion detonated from whatever game was on the screen beyond his phone. He tapped tapped away, playing.

I halfway wished I could take back my joke.

Sometimes the fact that my family had money and Justice was on scholarship came up suddenly and sucked the air out of our conversations, leaving smoke between us. He asked stuff like two years still wasn't enough for him to stop testing whether I was really down or just fake down.

I mean, I get it. I'm like (nearly) everybody at Flowered Arms Academy—my parents are ballers. They own Flexx Unlimited, a hip-hop lifestyle and media company. They've been influencers since before it was a thing thing. But that's where how I'm like other Flo-A Magnolias ends. Being cluelessly privileged ain't gonna get it in my house.

I bet nobody else's family ever went back to their "roots" like mine did. If they even had roots that weren't dirty rich. A lot of Mag families had been wealthy a long time. Our money was so new, there were still people at Flo-A who believed the rumor that my parents had created Flexx from drug money.

The point is, I was a Mag, but I wasn't.

And Jus was the same way.

He was Mr. Ball So Hard, but scholarship kids were

low in our school's pecking order. Even the popular ones. It was the Flo way. Me copping to being spoiled was a reminder he didn't need. I was relieved when he broke the silence.

"I saw in the chat Sammie working at the Haven. What you getting into this summer?"

Sammie was my cousin Samej. Her dad and my mom were brother and sister. Yes, Samej is her dad's name (James) spelled backward. And yes, she will read you if you feel the need to comment on it. Don't say it's interesting. Don't say it's weird. Just don't say.

Sammie was a year older than me and lived a block away from Justice in Marks Park. She was the older sister neither me or Justice had. Love it or hate it. I loved that me and him had that connection outside of just knowing each other from school. It made me even less Flo.

I had absolutely no plans this summer, since Sammie dropped a pic of the front of Burger Haven with the words—guess I be smelling like beef and sweat all summer—in the group chat she had with me and Justice. The second she turned fifteen, Uncle James had her putting in job applications. Now it was official. No kicking it this summer.

I flipped the question back to him. "Are you playing for Rico's team again?"

We were both playing a game because he went on like I hadn't asked about his usual summer league gig. "Ay, what you know about Style High?"

He ogled me through the screen, eyebrows knitted.

I knitted mine right back, in legit bewilderment. "What's Style High?"

"Yo, it's a bad look that I know more about something going on at Flexx then you do," he said, laughing.

It wasn't saying anything that people knew a lot about my parents' company. There was a lot of pride in District City that a company known worldwide was in their backyard.

I waved him off and ran my finger lovingly over the picture I was drawing—a pair of genie pants with a bandeau top. The tight top with the flowy pants was an opposites attract love fest. This was definitely making my Wall of Hall of all of my best design sketches.

Okay, that name sounds wild. Hall stands for Hot and Litty Lit. My best friend Rachel named it. For real, it's corny. But she wouldn't stop calling it that. So, it stuck.

The genie pants would have plenty of competition, since the Wall of Hall was probably going to be full by the end of the summer. Sketching was how I chilled. I didn't have anything but time this summer.

Justice's voice floated my way. "So you really don't know anything about it?"

"Style High," I repeated, shaking my head.

"It's a summer fashion program," he said. "They're looking for trainees. I saw the application for it at the Marks rec center awhile back."

My hand stopped abruptly, making one of the shirt's bands darker in one spot than the rest.

Style High.

Fragments of memory floated from one part of my brain to another, falling into place like a jigsaw puzzle, remembering how Daddy had seen some article about this sixteen-year-old designer. He'd reminisced about how the dude was just like him at that age. How kids from District City's working-class communities needed to know that there were other ways to success that didn't involve sports.

My father always has a million ideas, all bursting to be born the second they come out of his mouth and most of them never seeing the light of day because he'd birth another one sometimes before the first thought was complete. I figured the night had ended like that.

I schooled myself at the Flexx web page about Style High, reading aloud like I was doing a commercial:

"'Flexx Unlimited is dedicated to exposing Black youth

from District City to opportunities designed to help them play a role in the evolution of hip-hop culture. Style High is a stipend-based competitive trainee program for rising ninth graders with a passion for fashion and styling.'"

I peered up at Justice. "Hold up. It pays?"

The glow from his game monitor lit up his face as he nodded eagerly.

"Shoot, maybe I should apply," I said, laughing.

"Like you need to work," he scoffed, not letting me get away with the joke.

My face was hot with embarrassment. He was right. But dang, he didn't have to call me out. I played it off. "It definitely sounds like something my father dreamed up. He's all about young talent." I closed the website and went back to the sketch that my heart wasn't in anymore.

Every time Justice said something about what I had or what my family had, it was like discovering a new pinhole in a big balloon that had to be patched. I was always desperate to find the words that could be slapped over the hole to stop the leak. This time, he did the patching.

"It sound clutch. I mean if you really get to style and stuff." He squinted at the camera. "Your pops pretty down. You think he'd make people be running crazy errands? Like testing you on what type of mocha latte chai he likes."

"First of all, my father doesn't drink fancy coffee," I said, glad for the easy breeze between us again. "Second, I don't see how that's training unless you want work at a coffeehouse. Third, I don't know what they would have people doing."

He grinned at me, so close to the camera it looked more like a brown face pie with whipped cream sprayed in the shape of a smile.

"Well . . ." He shook the piece of paper at the screen. "I applied."

"Then why you frontin' like you didn't know about it?" I said.

His lips crimped. He returned the eye roll without answering.

"My bad." I nodded. "The rules."

He spat back. "The rules, yeah." His voice softened. "At least you admit they exist."

My heart raced, stupidly happy at the compliment.

One point for really down.

Flo-A had a lot of rules that nobody ever admitted were rules.

Like, if you came from money and asked someone else from money for a favor or a hookup, it was networking. But if you didn't have money and asked for that same favor, you were a gopher. That's what Mags called anybody who they felt were digging for clout or status.

I'd seen it happen before—a student on scholarship forgetting they weren't really one of "us" approaching somebody they thought was a friend for a favor, and then suddenly they're iced out of invites to places like they had a disease.

I kept my eyes on my sketch, afraid they'd betray my hurt if I looked at him. "You could have told me you were applying."

His laugh felt forced. "I figured. But I ain't want you to feel like you needed to hook me up." There was a tiny pause, then it was like he pushed the question out with all the air in his lungs. "So is it against the rules that I'm trying get a hookup at your pops' company?"

His mouth pooched, defiantly, like he was waiting for me to whip out a book and check for confirmation.

I pretended to think about it before being honest. "It's only a problem if you worried about people thinking you a gopher."

"Man, I ain't stuntin' what nobody think," he said. "Except you." His eyes shifted right then left like he was looking into mine instead of a tiny camera at the top of a phone. "I want it to be cool with you."

"I'm cool with it," I said, loving that I was the only person at Flo-A whose opinion he cared about.

He seemed to bounce now that the news was out.

"Good. 'Cause for real, I already got offered the position."

I slammed the pencil down on my pad. "So much for worrying about how I feel about it, Jus."

He teased. "You mad?"

Not mad. Hurt.

I get it. He didn't want the hookup.

I opened my mouth to ask. Then stopped.

I didn't want the air sucked out of the room anymore. My voice went up a few notches.

"I'm not, though. For real." I cheesed at him. "I'm the only one who knows you got sketch skills anyway."

His head bobbed up and down, confirming his secret talent was still that. Warmth spread around me like a blanket, again. I stayed quiet as he confessed.

"Keeping it a stack, I wanted to mention it to you so many times. I know people at school gonna think you hooked me up, regardless. But I ain't tripping. I got this on my own."

A fierce need to protect him raced through me. "And I got your back if somebody try come for you over it."

His eyes flickered away from the screen and to me, like there was more. I waited a few seconds, then finally reached toward the screen to end the call.

"All right, then. I still got studying to do. I'll holler at you later."

He hollered out, "Mari, Mari, Mari . . . wait."

I peered into the screen, wondering if the wind would blow—hot or cool. "Huh?"

"Happy friendversary," he said, then beat me to the punch hanging up.

CHAPTER .2.

I dropped a message into the chat I had with my parents:
Hello? When was someone going to tell
me that Justice was down with Flexx
this summer? 🫣 😐

I took a notepad and my thick World Hist book downstairs and studied in the kitchen.

If I stayed in my room, I'd tuck myself away in the window seat that overlooked a small patch of trees and sketch all night. Tomorrow was the last day of school, and finals mattered at Flo-A.

I shook my head at the message that rang in.

Daddy:
New phone who dis? Cause it can't

be my daughter b/c she NEVER
asks what's happening at the
company her parents started to
make sure she don't have to hustle
the way they did.

Mommy:

Daddy is so dramatic. Lol You never
asked, luv-luv. Jus never told you?

Mari_Golden:

Soooo dramatic. Not til just now.

Daddy:

Ganging up on me. Wow. Don't
come for me, ladies. 💪

Me and mommy rang in with the identical eye rolling
emoji.

Daddy:

But good for him! Applying for the
program was his business.

Mari_Golden:

Okay daddy. Well, he's super psyched
about it.

Daddy:

He should be. Over 120 kids

applied and we only picked three.

And ol Yes Sir was one of them.

Yes Sir was Daddy's nickname for Justice, because those were usually the only words he said when he was over. He could talk for hours to Ms. Sadie and even around my mom he was fine. But the second Daddy walked in, it was—"Yes sir, school is good. Yes sir, I think we gonna have a good season."

I swore one day Daddy was going to mess up and call him that instead of his name.

I peaced out of our chat and settled in to study.

Our kitchen took up the whole back of the second floor of our townhouse. The big center island could seat six. In the rear was a table surrounded by four high-backed wooden chairs against a big bay window that looked out into our small backyard. A giant shiny metal hood seemed ready to inhale the stove. The way it vacuumed scents out of the room was the only reason our house didn't smell like stale oil from all of Ms. Sadie's frying. Still, it was like studying in a soul food library.

The salty scent of our fried-pork-chop dinner clung to the air.

Thirty minutes later, Ms. Sadie shuffled in, on a mission. She had on a pair of fleece pajamas and a robe, closed up like it was below zero in the house. Without ever looking my way, she headed to the fridge. She rummaged through it, tiny and hunched over, then plucked out a can of ginger ale.

If she was five feet tall, I was the Queen of England. For being so small, she could smack good and hard if she needed to. A little slice of discipline I hadn't experienced in forever, since I usually obeyed after the first warning when her eyes went beady and her lips pressed together until they disappeared.

Ms. Sadie wasn't blood. She raised my dad when my real grandmother died and had as much influence over what I got to do or not do as my parents. Sometimes it felt like more.

"You going to bed already?" I asked.

She raised up, surprised, head whipping my way.

"What you mean, already?" Ms. Sadie could scold the sun out of the sky. It was her way, like a dog barking but never biting. "It's nine o'clock. Some of us turn in at a decent hour. Maybe if you didn't spend so much time talking to that little boy, you could be in bed yourself, then be up and ready to get at the day by five."

"Nobody but you and Daddy want to get at anything at five in the morning."

"Young people got all the energy in the world. Y'all the ones that should be able to get up early and keep going," she said, fussing without any bite. "How that little boy doing?"

She knew Justice's name just fine and liked him.

She didn't condone any type of boyfriends. And after she mentioned it a million times, to my total embarrassment, that I was too young to date, she figured he got the message. Justice acted like it was normal that somebody would repeat the same speech over and over for two months straight. I guess the lecture was the price he paid for her cooking, which he loved. Fact was, if somebody was a friend of mine, they better show their face around 1412 Lee Street.

I was secretly grateful for the rule. It helped me and Jus go from school friends to real friends. That and the fact that there were only five Black dudes at Flo-A to begin with. Not five in my grade, five in the whole entire school. If we want to get real about why I probably won't have a boyfriend until I'm grown, it's because of that.

Also, those five dudes are spread out good, like Flo-A's trustee board was afraid if they admitted a bunch of Black boys the same age they'd go Nat Turner on the administration.

There was Darrod and Rolani, both too old for me.

Cute little Peter, who was in third grade. And will probably break many hearts once he's in upper school.

And Milton, who thinks he's White because he's on the golf team. Or maybe is on the golf team because he thinks he's White. I don't know which. He's heading to ninth grade like me and Justice, but pretends we're invisible if we're ever anywhere near each other. Like our Blackness will rub off on him if he speaks to us.

Once Justice realized that I wasn't anything like Milton, we were good. And once he tasted Ms. Sadie's cooking, our friendship was sealed—'cause not like he could get smothered turkey legs and macaroni and cheese at one of the other basketball players' houses.

I dug back playfully.

"Justice is fine. He also just told me he's working at Flexx this summer." I made a zero with my fingers. "I now have this many people to hang out with once school ends tomorrow."

The thought settled into the pit of my stomach. Saying it to somebody else made it hit different. It also made me realize I never had that many choices to begin with, without Samej.

I only ever saw Justice a few times over the summer. When me and Samej caught a few of his games or if he and his mother dropped into church.

And Rachel always had a summer camp on tap. One year it was cinematography camp. Another it was a STEAM camp and she complained about it so much her parents had to go get her early. This year, she was going to be a junior counselor at a track camp. And by counselor, I mean her parents still had to pay for her to go. But I guess she had a little bit of authority since all the other campers were in elementary school.

Ms. Sadie pulled out the high-back chair next to me and, with some effort, stepped on the rung at the bottom, gripping the back with one gnarled hand and steadying her other hand on the table.

It reminded me that she was old. Seventy-five, this year. And I hated it.

It didn't matter how bossy she was. Or that she always vetoed me going to the "biggest" party of the year. Or that it was usually an automatic no for the overnight ski or beach getaways school friends invited me to. I couldn't imagine life without her.

The thought that one day it would just be me and my parents made my stomach quiver. I hugged myself, pretending like I felt the cold she always did, and waited for her to settle into the chair comfortably.

"You be fine," Ms. Sadie said. She lifted her head, checking my notes. "Your studies going good?"

The gentle husk of her voice blanketed me, reminding me the future without her was a dream and all that mattered was she was still here.

"They're going okay." I scribbled a smiley face in the margin of my notepad to assure myself of the answer. Glad for the distraction, I went on telling her more than she probably wanted to hear about how hard Mr. Maroney had made our final.

She waved in the general direction of my notebook. "I already know how smart you are. Those grades about proving to them that you smart."

"Them" were the faculty and other parents at Flo-A. Ms. Sadie didn't have much patience for either. "Too many rules that don't have nothing to do with nothing but keeping that school the way it was when it started," is what she'd always say if I came home with a memo about some new morality code or mandatory change to uniform.

I appreciated her version of sympathy, but I cared about my grades. As if reading my mind, she fussed on. "Pea Head and Nut think I don't understand why they sent you to a private school. I do." She nodded like my parents were there needing confirmation. "They want you to have a smoother road than they did. But the company already making more money than your grandchildren can spend. That'll make the road pretty smooth, if you ask me." She ran her hand across the table, then looked at her fingers, inspecting for dust. There wouldn't be any. She kept the kitchen spotless. "I'm glad you getting a education, Mari Henny, but there's a whole lot just being part of the world can teach you."

I bit back the breath wanting to fly out of my mouth in frustration.

They kept me volunteering in Marks Park and dragged me to every photo shoot to smile beside the big checks they donated to programs in need to remind me that the rest of the world was different from the strict and sometimes mindlessly White standards of Flo-A.

I was already "part of the world," forever stuck between life at school and home where it was Marks Parks mentality in a T-Hill zip code.

I code switch so much, I can teach a class.

And you know what the world had taught me so far? That it's mad tiring when you not Black enough for some people and too Black for other people.

If I said any of that to Ms. Sadie, she would say I wasn't grateful.

I scribbled, "but I am," in my notebook as she said, "It's none of my business—"

I groaned.

Nothing good ever followed those words.

"It's none of my business but . . ."

That child don't need that many shoes.

Mari don't need to be jetting off to California and missing school to attend no awards show with y'all.

I kept my eyes on my notepad waiting on the latest thing she was going to give advice on that "wasn't" her business.

"No. I'm serious now," Ms. Sadie said, her wrinkled face solemn. "Sammie got a job, now. What you plan to do this summer?"

The question was a trap. Hanging with my cousin Sammie wasn't all fun. The free time we got had always been earned by helping at one of Bethlehem United's programs at least three times a week—food ministry, youth ministry, vacation Bible school. There was a ministry for every week of summer, minus the two my parents took us on vacation.

My plans for the summer? Whatever new ministry was out there waiting on me as Ms. Sadie's obedient hand girl.

I scoffed. "Wait, I got a choice?"

The disappointment in her face made her grayish blue eyes look cloudy.

"You always got a choice, Mari Henny." She pursed her lips at my look of doubt. "Just 'cause you don't like the choices don't mean you don't got 'em."

"I don't know what I'm doing," I said, wishing she'd just tell me where she had already promised me and get it over with. I scribbled "Marks Hill" until the pen scratched through the page. Ms. Sadie waited on a better answer that I didn't have. I didn't know what she wanted me to say and didn't feel like pretending I did.

If this was a regular summer, the second I walked off school grounds, District City was me and Samej's playground: going back and forth between each other's houses for sleepovers; hosting our own reality shows; talking to boys from her school late into the night pretending I was from out of state (my Southern accent got better each year); hanging out in the park, me drawing and her writing; and hooking up with her friends who adopted me as their little tagalong cousin with the Flexx connect to concerts and listening parties.

Summer was when I didn't have to remember which Flo-A rule to follow.

This wasn't a regular summer.

Somehow I'd gotten left out of the meeting where everybody decided this was the year they would play grown-up and get jobs. I felt blindsided. Ms. Sadie's eagle-eyed stare made it worse.

I blurted nonsense.

"It's not like y'all ever let me go with my school friends when they be asking me to go to their summer houses." I sucked my teeth, dangerously close to being disrespectful, but on a roll. "I mean used to ask me. Nobody invite me anymore 'cause they know y'all gonna say no." A fact that only stopped hurting once me and Justice started getting closer.

Calm as ever, Ms. Sadie retorted, "You spend enough time as it is with all them White kids. I would think you as tired of complaining about how persnickety they are as I am of hearing about it. Summer your chance to be around your own."

She wasn't wrong, but I was the one who had to hear about all the plans being made, see the pics posted on everybody's Buzz account, then hear about how much fun it had been the first few weeks when school reopened. Not caring was hard when it was always in my face.

I went on more pout than rant. "I don't have no

problem being around my own. Y'all always make sure of that. So just tell me where I'm volunteering this summer." That got an eyebrow raise out of her. I brought it home, complete with folding my arms like I was a two-year old. "I already know I'm stuck here in the house until you, Mommy, and Daddy decide to send me on a missionary trip to Africa to build schools or dig a well."

She locked eyes with me, slicing through my tirade.

"I don't know about no trip to Africa. But ain't nothing wrong with spending the summer doing more than staying up all night whispering into the phone to God knows who."

So much for me and Samej thinking we'd kept our late-night calls quiet. She ignored the surprise on my face.

"I been thinking." Her cool soft hand covered mine. "Ask your momma and daddy about what you can do at the company this summer?"

My head jerked up like it had been lifted by a string.

"Style High?" I asked.

She gently fed me crumbs. "That's that new program your little friend in, right?"

I nodded, not bothering to ask how she knew about all that. When my parents made it to a meal, "shop talk" was strictly prohibited at Ms. Sadie's dinner table. Yet somehow she seemed to know things. I never knew how much until times like this.

I couldn't tell if she was the messenger or the mastermind, this time.

"Is this what y'all had planned for me?" I treaded carefully, curious. "How come no one ever mentioned it before?"

Ms. Sadie's right eyebrow arched so high the wrinkles around her eye smoothed to baby fineness. "Do it need to be anybody's plan? You waiting on an invitation to be something other than spoiled?"

I had been all ready to admit that Style High had me curious. That I was down for a summer hanging out in the halls of Flexx instead of the dim, musty bowels of Beth United. Then she went and used the S word.

"I'm not spoiled," I said automatically.

High-key, the word triggers me.

Spoiled people got their way all the time. Trust, that was not me.

Ms. Sadie felt otherwise.

She looked at me long and hard. Her hand squeezed mine, holding firm as she talked.

"You think doing what you told mean you ain't spoiled?"

I didn't answer and still her head nodded in deep

affirmation as if she'd come to terms with the fact that she and I weren't going to see eye to eye.

"I ain't gonna argue what spoiled is or ain't." Her mouth wrenched in distaste. "But it sound like even your little friends have enough sense to start thinking about what the future hold beyond getting their nails done or bouncing a ball. Getting a job at the company 'bout as easy as opening your eyes each morning."

She eased her way out of the chair, scolding all the way, finger wagging in my face.

"I ain't think summers was that hard on your butt, from the get-go. Giving a couple hours a day to the church ain't a hard time by a long shot." Her voice lost its bite. She stood beside my chair, her arm around its back. "I'll miss having your help. So will Pastor. But I think it'll do you good to be in this new program with kids, Black kids, who got that eye like you do." She squeezed my arm playfully. "If you not interested, then I got plenty keep you busy."

With a light pat to my side, she shuffled off.

CHAPTER .3.

The next day, the sweet words of "Have a nice summer" signaled my freedom and release from my chains as an eighth grader. People had zero chill. They ran through the halls, singing, laughing, shouting, "accidentally" missing the bin as they trashed fat binders full of notes.

Because it wasn't just the last day, it was Crossing Day, when the eighth graders walked over the bridge that separated the elementary/middle buildings from the high school. It was our unofficial entry into the upper school. Crossing Day was corny. It was also one of the many traditions that made Flo-A what it was and an annual rite of passage that every single Flo-A student took seriously. There had already been a whole week of assemblies and ceremonies to mark our promotion, but this was the day we all cared about.

As we flocked outside, Rachel grabbed my arm. "Come to Moe's. I leave for track camp soon. It's probably the last day I'll get to hang out."

She pulled her thick strawberry blonde hair into a ponytail. We barely had to move. The flow of traffic carried us through the hall.

"The crazy thing is I'm looking forward to it," she said, all grins. "It's this place up in the hills of New York. I don't even know if the internet works up there."

Leave it to Rachel to think no Wi-Fi was roughing it. But I played along.

"Wait. What? No Wi-Fi? Girl, you're nuts."

She laughed, gripping my arm tighter as the crowd pushed us together.

Rachel was my girl. Had been since fourth grade when we got paired for a science project and realized neither one of us would ever be a scientist. Seriously, her parents should have seen the STEAM camp debacle coming a mile away. She didn't take herself or Flo-A seriously even though she was a legacy.

Her dad was an 88 and she was a 112. In other words, he was in the 88th graduating class of the school and

Rachel would be the 112th. Most Legs were pressed over their status. Not Rachel.

She talked in excited bursts about what it would be like to be with Alex, her boyfriend and a long-distance runner, without any adults around. I didn't bother to remind her there would be real actual adults that got paid as counselors there, too.

Our bodies moved in sync with the crowd as we headed down the long winding sidewalk that ran along the side of the school toward the wooden bridge that divided the lower school campus from the upper school side.

Members of the basketball team rushed past us. They moved with a swiftness that caught up anybody near them until everybody was moving even faster.

A long oval-shaped lake glistened, guiding us out of the path. Willow trees clustered on one end. On the other end, a small grassy hill sloped down from the administration building.

Our loud voices broke up the area's peace.

Soon-to-be seventh graders stood back, close to the school, watching the spectacle—careful not to come near the bridge on a day meant only for us. Crossing Day was one of those things that everybody looked forward to. And for a long time, I had too. But Justice's text, from earlier, had me feeling mixed about it.

Why we excited to cross a bridge? We
gon be in 9th grade next year whether
we do it or not. I just meet u there.

He had ignored my question—
If you gonna be on the bridge anyway
why not walk w/ everybody? 😒

Rachel finally took a breath from her rambling. "Where's Justice?"

I pointed. "Already on the bridge. He asked me to meet him here."

Justice stood in the middle, leaning on the railing. Some people gave him a pound as they passed. He obliged, nonchalantly, letting the crowd race by him.

Rachel squealed. "Maybe he's ready to make you guys' little thing official. I'll need deets," she said in my ear as she gave me a squeeze, then let the sea of students carry her away.

My heart skittered at the prospect of Justice asking me to be his girlfriend.

Us being a couple made total sense. The lies I'd be telling if I said I hadn't thought about it. But, in a way, we were closer than some couples. Justice was legit the first boy to step to me and clown about how things worked at our school. Whenever we talked, it was like finally being able to laugh about a joke that only you had been in on forever. He was in on how stupid Flo-A's rules were and how our friends' cool was corny.

And once he met my family, he got that I was in on it, too. The privileges I had because my parents have money made me like everybody else at school, but come two thirty, when that bell rang, I had to leave all that on campus. At home, that private school mess did not fly. He knew that how I was at school, wasn't how I was at home.

I needed that more than I wanted a boyfriend.

The crowd flowed fast, like a river. As it thinned out, Justice withdrew from the pounds, nods, and calls of "Have a good summer, J-Free." Head down, looking at his phone, his long finger skating across the screen.

He was already changed and looking fresh in a pair of black-and-white plaid shorts, white tennas, and a clean, crisp white T-shirt. He hated that I called his shoes tennas. "That sounds country," he always teased. But words mean things. He had on tennis shoes and that's what I called them. To me, kicks were the things he wore to play basketball. Either way, he kept them all clean like they were precious metal.

Then here I come, looking haggard and tired in my

well-worn uniform: a white polo, a black-gold-and-white plaid skort, and my only individual touch—a pair of open-toed, strappy sandals that would have gotten me a dress code vio if it weren't the last day.

Once I'd gotten his text to meet him, I'd been too anxious to change. I wanted to tell him about me joining Style High. Well, that I wanted to. I hadn't asked my parents yet. But I couldn't see them saying no.

His head popped up when he registered me standing in front of him. He waited until the last of our classmates had gone by before saying, "That was cornbally as hell. But at least security didn't bother me today." He nodded in the direction of an officer at the bridge's end giving everyone who played along a high five. "It's a trip that they not out here directing traffic when a whole-ass class crossing the bridge. But I stand out here by myself and they on me asking for my ID."

"You're out of uniform, soldier," I joked, dropping my tote onto the bench beside him. "They think you don't belong."

He snorted. "Who said I do belong?"

It was my turn to snort. "Yeah, well, if you don't belong you fake it good."

He dropped his phone into his shorts pockets, folded

his arms. "Whatever. They need to go 'head with that wack profiling. It's not a lot of us here. They should at least recognize us when they see us."

That was pie-in-the-sky thinking and he knew it. Flo-A's officers weren't rent-a-cops. They were the school's private police force that guarded the twenty-acre campus like it was a small city.

In uniform, you blended in and they tended to mostly ignore you unless you were violating one of the many rules. Out of uniform you were fair game. It was the Flo-A way. If he'd been White and standing there out of uniform, just five minutes after the school bell, security would have still made him produce ID.

I didn't feel like having that debate.

School was out and I could breathe for the first time since exams started.

Justice kept going, riled up.

"Even if I wasn't a student, what am I hurting just standing here looking at water and ducks?" He challenged me like I was head of security. "They act like the only people that be thieving and robbing are non-students. Puh. Please."

Usually we bonded over griping about Flo-A's hokey traditions and book of rules. Today felt different.

I perched at the edge of the bench, looking up at him until he was done venting.

"You all right?" I asked.

"Yeah. Why?" He frowned.

"You're going off, for real," I said.

"Sometimes I just get sick of the bull." He crossed his ankles, staring over my head to the forest of willows. "I grin and play ball for them all semester. Get them as close to the Regents as their sorry butts been in three years. And security don't even recognize me?"

"Oh, you mad because they don't ask for your autograph," I teased.

"I'm serious, Marigold." His eyes rolled. "Don't you ever get sick of playing the game? Everybody here try to act like race don't matter. But who security gonna stop first? Me or Andy Winchester?"

"Jus, you know how serious they are about that. Even if they saw a family—Black or White—walking the campus, they'd escort them to Admin for a visitors' badge." I shrugged. "It's just how they are."

"You believe that?" He shook his head like he pitied me. "You really think a White family would be pulled up and escorted to get a badge? Pssh."

"I don't know, Jus," I said, choosing the easy way out

of the rising tension between us. "I'm just glad to be done, for real."

"You got that right." He smoothed at his eyebrows. "I'm ready for a break from this place and people who act like they're just tolerating me." He turned back toward the water, leaning over the bridge's railing. "This is my second private school since fourth grade." He threw something into the water. It plunked quietly and sent a few droplets onto my bare legs. "Another scholarship always waiting for me somewhere else. Flo-A better act like they know."

Talk of him moving to another school got me to my feet. I joined him at the railing and changed the subject.

"I didn't know Style High was only three trainees. My father must think you have skills, boyee."

His face lit up.

"He recognized," he said, before laughing sheepishly. "I gotta keep it a stack, I was nervous at the interview. Even though I been at your house and know your pops, it was mad weird having him ask me questions like that. But he was crazy cool. We talked about where hip-hop fashion going. He asked how I defined my own style. Was I a style leader or follower . . ."

His voice trailed as he looked off. There was a glow of

happiness on his face. I'd seen that look a million times before but never on Justice.

He was a fanboy. Most people from DC were.

If he'd acted like that early in our friendship, I'm not sure we would have ever become friends. It wasn't that I thought he was a gopher, but hello, if I thought he was just friends with me because of who my father was . . .

Nope. Nah. I can't fade that.

I was glad that wasn't the case. It couldn't have been. This was the first time Justice was openly giddy about my father. I couldn't resist joking him.

"Look at you. Mad props for holding in your Flexx fanboy love for so long."

His grin spread. "I'm stanning like a mug, right?"

"A little bit. But go on and brag. Daddy said they had 120 applications."

His eyes widened, then he quickly got his chill back. "I can't wait." He edged closer to me, our arms touching, making me want to stay that way. "Mainly 'cause it's gonna be that shizz. But also to get away from these bougie ass gringos for a while."

"Please tell me you plan to stop using that word this summer. It's rude and low-key racist," I said, but couldn't help smiling at the devilish grin on his face.

"Maybe I will. Maybe I won't."

He started in again, shattering the mood.

"I'm over this place, man."

I was kind of over the whole conversation, but I stayed close, hoping the storm would blow over. My arm vibrated a little as the muscles in his arm trembled while he ranted.

"For real, I don't even know if I'll be back to Flo-A next year."

My neck snapped back.

"Why not?" I asked, hating the high-pitched alarm in my voice.

I sat down on the bench so I could get a good look at him and because my legs felt stiff like I was on stilts and ready to nose-dive.

For a second, a shadow passed over his face.

Justice had a big nose, but because he was always smiling you could ignore it. With his eyes narrowed, his perfect fineness was flawed by the puff of his nose.

His head shook side to side as the words spewed, slowly at first, then in a rush.

"The dean is mad that I'm doing Style High instead of playing summer league ball. He didn't say he was taking my scholarship away but he may as well have." He did a dead-on impression of Dean Whitmore. "'Mr. Freeman, our understanding was that basketball was something you took seriously. Someone who takes their craft seriously must hone that craft. Summer league is your best option to stay in top condition and be ready for the season. There's a very good chance you'll make varsity. A rarity for a freshman.'" Justice's eyes rolled. "He act like I need him to tell me how to stay in shape. I work out every day in season or off. Every day."

He silently glowered over my head at the bank of willows behind me.

"Is doing summer league part of your pledge?" I asked.

"Not exactly," he said. "It says I have to stay in shape and if I'm not season ready my scholarship could be revoked. But they scouted me from summer league, so they just assumed I'd always do it. Like I'm a trained monkey or something."

All scholarship students signed a commitment pledge. Daddy hated them. He said they were contracts in disguise and that it wasn't right that scholarship kids got locked into things that other players on the team didn't. I agreed, but I didn't want Justice to transfer. I tried to make a bright side.

"I'm sure they don't think that, Jus." I stood up. "You're the best player and—"

I froze a few inches from him as he barked at me.

"Mari, you don't know how it is. Yeah, you got rules you gotta follow here, but trust me you don't know the half of it." He smoothed at his eyebrows again, in long angry swipes.

Part of me wanted to say, Honor the contract. Not for the dean's sake, for mine. I didn't want to think about going into upper school without him. Especially now. The cliques were set. All I'd ever had was Rachel. And I was okay with that. But it was because I had Justice, too.

I poked, cautiously. "What's so bad about playing summer league?"

His sharp laugh cut through the lake's silence. Two ducks nearby flapped in panic until they realized there was no danger.

"Nothing's bad about summer league." He jutted his chin out. "But ain't nobody else gonna make me play if I don't want to play."

"But if it puts your pledge in danger, why not just do it?" I whispered, even though the bridge was empty except for us.

"Is that all you think I can do, Marigold?"

His voice was full of hurt, like he already knew the answer.

I touched his arm, thankful he didn't pull back.

"I'm not saying that. You always talked like summer league is better than school ball because your competition is tougher and . . ." I paused, not sure if I should go on. Knew I had to, because he'd be real if I was the one that needed a talk. "Plus, you said you made good money playing with Rico's."

"I did. But I guess it never occurred to nobody that I'd be anything but a baller. Huh?" His voice never rose. It didn't have to. He came at me hard. "I thought you got it. But you like everybody else, just worried about making sure I do what they brought me here to do."

He slung his backpack over his shoulder. His words were icy.

"I don't have no senator father like some people here. I can't be daddy's aide one day for the summer. Or work for his law firm. I don't even speak to my father." He snorted in disgust. "Whether the dean like it or not, I got choices." He talked past me to the willows, his jaw tight. "You know what the tripping part is? If anybody else had told the dean they'd gotten a program with one of the top companies in the country, he would have been proud as a new father."

His face tensed while that thought struck him somewhere deep. Then just as quickly, his face went blank like a light had been turned off. "But I forgot. I'm not just anybody else."

He gave me a curt nod.

"Look I hit you up, later. My moms got me running some errands for her."

Without another word he walked off.

CHAPTER .4.

The thumping in my head didn't stop until I walked through the door.

Daddy was home. Had to be, the house smelled like all his favorites—brown gravy, beef, and cabbage that had been slow-cooking all day. It was early June and Ms. Sadie was cooking like it was November. That meant she was in her world, having somebody to cook too much for.

I threw my bag on the floor and wasn't even a step away from it when Ms. Sadie came out the kitchen, fast on her seventy-five-year-old legs. She was dressed in her chef's whites—a white dress, white apron, white stockings and white nurse's shoes with the thick soles. She wore them to cook for Bethlehem United's homeless program.

When she moved in with us, her only job was to help raise me, but she insisted on cleaning our three-level townhouse and cooking every meal. My parents finally forced her to stop cleaning when she turned seventy. She didn't talk to them for a week. Now she spent all her time at Beth U because, in her words, what in the world was she supposed to do in this big house if she wasn't keeping it clean?

I guess relaxing never crossed her mind.

Her eyes may have been old, but they didn't miss anything. She peered at me, staring in my face like it was a book she'd read before. I fought emotions, trying not to look upset.

"Who you been fussing with now? That little blonde girl who don't got no manners?" I hadn't been friends with Lana since sixth grade, but Ms. Sadie still had thoughts about her. My frown only made her more stern. "Umhm. Or probably with that little boy." She shook her head. "That's probably it. You too young to be dating, anyway. But tell him come on by soon. He the only one I know, besides Marshall, that eat like a real person. You and Nut act like you always on a diet."

We didn't. We couldn't help that Ms. Sadie cooked like she was in the army. Even if I ate two plates, it didn't put a dent in what was left over. Daddy ate like he was starving, but then he also got up at five a.m. every day to work out with his personal trainer.

I mustered up enough energy to play along.

"Ms. Sadie, nobody dating nobody." The truth sucked me even deeper into my feelings. I forced cheer into my voice. "But I'll be sure to let Justice know you expect a visit." I pecked her cheek.

She hunched her shoulders. "Who? He not coming here to see me." She kissed me back, then pointed at the bag. "Unah. Pick that up and put it in that closet."

"Is Daddy here?" I peered toward his home office.

"Yeah, he here, but try walking out this foyer without picking up that bag and see what happen," she said, confident I'd obey.

I grabbed it, slung it into the closet, and raced into my father's office.

My mother sat, legs crossed at the feet, in her first lady's chair in front of Daddy's big antique wood desk. She was still dressed for work in a peach-colored jacket with big belled sleeves that stopped at her elbows and was cropped to just under her breast. She looked like a well-dressed butterfly that had just landed.

I dutifully pecked her on the lips before throwing myself into Daddy's arms.

"Daddy's girl," she said under her breath.

"All day," I teased back, loving the feel of Daddy's embrace.

I was a daddy's girl for sure, and it was mostly her doing. She was the one that had always made sure we video called when he was away. She was the one who scooped me up from school and arranged for us to have dinner in his office at Flexx if too many evenings had gone by without me seeing him. The one who had archived a lifetime's worth of video and pictures of me and Daddy preparing for and heading off to Flo-A's annual Father-Daughter Ball.

She'd never had a relationship with her father, so I guess making sure I had one with mine was the next best thing.

"Hi, Daddy." I relished the tight squeeze a few minutes, then pulled back long enough to kiss his cheek. "I didn't know you were back."

"Yep. A few hours ago, but I stopped by the office first." He pulled a box from beneath his chair, anticipating my next question. "It's a kimono top." He beamed at me. "We're calling it the Flexxin' Kimo Crop."

I tore into the shiny box and snatched out a silky white half shirt that wrapped, with large sleeves that ended in a pocket. A thin string of light and dark pink blossoms hung off a green vine that ran up, down, and around the whole top. I held it up to me. "Ooh, it's adorable."

He clapped his hands together and rambled excitedly. "This is just the prototype. They're working on making it out of less expensive material for me. But it's something I want to offer to one of the new young groups we end up styling . . . get some buzz going."

I did a quick turn, letting him fawn over me.

"It's hot," I said, laying it in its nest of pink tissue.

He sat back in his big chair. "How were exams?" He laughed at the face I made. "That bad?"

I sank into the chair next to Mommy's and played up my sorrow.

"Send me to public school next year."

"You'd never survive, baby girl," my mother said with a wry smile.

"Nah. Marigold's tougher than you give her credit for, Nut," my father said. He rocked in his seat, hands folded on his chest, taking inventory of me. "But be careful what you ask for. I wouldn't mind saving the guap I drop in tuition each year."

He and my mother shared a chuckle at my expense.

"You just might if I didn't pass my World Hist exam," I said.

They knew I wasn't really in danger of failing. The school would have alerted them weeks ago. But they nodded sympathetically anyway.

I repositioned the chair so I could see both their faces.

"I want to work at Flexx this summer," I said.

The idea, only a seed the night before, had blossomed the second Justice mentioned transferring. What if he didn't return in the fall?

My father put his hand to his ear. "Did you say you wanted to wuh . . ." He fake struggled with the word. "Wu . . . work?"

Asking to work was pretty un-Marigold-like. But I was loving the thought more. The energy at Flexx was one part backstage at an awards show and one part hip-hop reality show. I could definitely do that for a few weeks.

"That's OD, Daddy," I said, taking the teasing in stride.

"Is it though?" he asked. "I mean, even with the volunteer work Mommy and Ms. Sadie put on you, your summers was way more chill than I ever had. I don't know if you're ready to work for me."

He started one of his many favorite stories about how he'd been hustling since he was eleven. Right as he got up to the part about helping his mother pay the light bills, Mommy—clearly out of patience—stepped in, "Marshall she's heard that a hundred times. So, you want to work. Which department?" She sat up in her chair, alert. One of her well-manicured eyebrows, already slightly arched, went up a notch. "And doing what? Do you expect to get paid?"

It never took my mother long to fall into what I called her Cee Oh Oh mode. She was Flexx's chief operating officer, which basically meant she ran things. All things. She did the same at home. Though, if I'm being honest, she was more of the Co-Cee Oh Oh with Ms. Sadie.

"Okay, Ma, there's this thing called an idea." I reached over and patted her hand "People get them, but they don't come with a lot of detail. Ever had one?"

My father died laughing. "She got you with that, Nut."

"No, she didn't get me." Her face worked hard not to smile. "That's totally you coming out of her, Marshall." She sat back in her chair, as if to say she was done, but kept right on lecturing. "Dreamers. Two peas in a pod. Always want to come up with the idea and then have somebody else work out the detail, also known as the important part. Hmph." Her butterfly sleeves fluttered as she spoke with her hands as much as with her mouth. "If you want to work at Flexx this summer, don't think you're going to come in and create your own position, hours and . . ." She

KEEPING IT REAL | 49

scowled. "Do you expect to get paid, Miss Girl?"

"Ma, of course." I scowled right back. "I said work, not volunteer."

"Oh, well then, definitely you're not going to be the one creating the terms," she said with finality.

"So, no big office with a window then?" I asked, pretending to take notes.

"Very funny, Marigold," she said, rolling her eyes. A smile fought to stay hidden on her lips.

I blew a kiss at her and she moved her head, dodging it.

As the frequent traveler, my father missed most of our debates. I think he enjoyed when we sparred. Caterwauling, Ms. Sadie called it.

I sat cross-legged in the chair, something that used to be really easy to do when I was little, but now nearly locked me into place between the chair's slim arms. My head ping-ponged between them, trying to catch their every word and reaction.

"Seriously. I was thinking I'd do Style High."

My mother's head whipped Daddy's way so fast, I wasn't sure who to look at. I chose her, which was probably the wrong choice because they were obviously having some sort of silent husband-wife conversation with their faces and I only caught half of it by looking at her. I didn't know what they were saying, but my mother's eyebrows were knitted tight, her lips pressed together.

Daddy came from around the desk and sat on its edge, between us. "You're not doing this to spend more time with that knucklehead, Justice, are you?"

My mouth worked with nothing but air coming out until the words squeaked through. "No. Why?"

Daddy snorted. "Because I think my baby girl has a crush." He stroked at the small patch of hair on his chin, squinted at me with a sly smile.

"Half the time Justice only be over here to help us eat all the food Ms. Sadie stay cooking." I smelled a no coming. Which I didn't get. I thought they'd be excited about me coming to them instead of them having to force me. I got serious. "Okay, so, I sort of got the idea from him. But it's not about him. Volunteering is cool when Sammie is with me. But I don't want do it alone."

I knew the admission wouldn't sit right with my mother since a lot of the volunteer work I did was helping her with her mentoring program. She jumped in.

"It shouldn't matter who does it with you, Marigold. Those programs depend on volunteers. You'll definitely be missed at the Diva program."

I don't think none of those girls would miss me. Some of them were fine. They loved Samej, for sure. Me? I was only two years older than them and I always got "she think she's cute" vibes from half of them. Mommy swore I was exaggerating. I wasn't.

"I can still help before school starts again," I said, politely avoiding dragging her darling divas. "And it's not just that anyway." I pulled out my secret weapon. "I've never been around other Black kids who into styling and designing." Daddy sat up straighter, letting me know I was onto something. "I probably would spend most of the summer drawing more designs anyway. I'd rather do it with other people who into it too."

Daddy clapped his hands once, loud. It meant an idea was brewing and he was excited about it. "You really want to do this, baby girl?"

"Marshall, let's talk about this first," my mother said. She sat at the edge of her chair, her face tight. "Remember we kept the program small for a reason. Four trainees is a lot to put on Marques and Joel on top of their other work."

Daddy wasn't pressed. "They'll be fine. Mari already know the industry. It's in her blood."

I nodded eagerly.

This was my chance to show Justice that I wasn't

spoiled and insensitive like other Mags. His words stabbed me in a place rarely poked—my pride.

I squirmed my way to the edge of my seat, trying but not being able to read the weird silence in the air.

I looked up at my father, head still cocked in thought. He nodded three times, then declared, "I think you doing Style High is an excellent idea. But look, we're bringing kids in for a real-world business experience. Nobody's going to treat you special, Mari. Can you deal with that?"

It was something Mommy would usually say. But I knew what answer was expected of me and I gave it. "Daddy, of course."

He looked to my mom for her final approval.

"Marigold, the kids selected for Style High are from some of DC's poorest neighborhoods," she said. I felt the rejection beneath her words. "I don't want to cheat them out of the full experience."

"Cheat them how?" I asked, annoyed that she was more worried about some random kids from the hood than me.

She sat up, fingers intertwined on her lap. No one and I mean no one could break bad news as rationally as my mother. You could have an airtight argument, but she had this way of talking like her idea was clearly the idea. Accept it. I prepared to pout as she explained.

"We created the program to give a certain type of student a chance. I'm worried you being involved might interfere with their freedom to speak and learn openly."

I slammed my back against the chair, but knew better than to fold my arms. "Wow, Ma, thanks for the support."

She scolded mildly.

"Don't do that, Marigold. This isn't about you right now. This program took months to engineer. We picked each candidate for specific reasons. You're asking us to add you at the last minute. I'm being clear that you're not just walking into this without it having implications."

Now I felt bad. I was mad at her for making me feel that way.

She reached over and stroked my hand gently.

I didn't snatch it away but wanted to.

"It's the last-minute element that bothers me," she said. Her eyes cut to my father.

I broke in, trying to stop whatever weird mind reading they did with each other.

"Okay, well, what if I still did something at Flexx, just not Style High?" I looked from one to the other. I wanted them to reject that idea and prayed they wouldn't call my bluff.

"Honestly, that might be easier," Mommy said, disappointing me.

"If you really want to get more involved in the family biz, we can find a way," Daddy said, basically agreeing. "Whatever we decide you gonna be good with."

His eyes locked onto mine. It wasn't a question.

I wanted to nod, but if they said no to Style High, I would be stuck doing who knew what.

I gave it another push. "It's just, that, Justice made Style High sound like a lot of fun. Where else could I be around a bunch of Black kids doing something like this?"

Just as Daddy seemed ready to agree, Mommy cut in. "True. We'll take that into consideration. But your request was to do something at Flexx this summer, correct?"

She had me with my own words. I quietly confirmed.

"Good. Let us look at the whole picture and get back to you," she said, firmly trying to dead the back and forth.

I looked to Daddy, debating if I should keep at it or leave my fate in his hands to battle it out with Mommy. I hadn't realized how much I wanted them to say yes, until I heard the words, "Let us get back to you."

I gave it one last try. I had to. My mother was too good at changing Daddy's mind.

"Okay." I stood up, stretching the kinks out of my legs,

like I was done, then said, "But let's be honest—is there anybody else more qualified to play a role in the evolution of hip-hop culture than moi? It's in my blood, right?"

I curtsied, hoping they didn't see the slight tremble in my leg as I played my last card.

Daddy's smile exploded, his light brown eyes gleaming.

"Somebody did their research," he said.

Feeling the tide turn, I rolled on. "I have my whole Wall of Hall if you need proof to show passion." Passion for fashion was Daddy's weak spot. "I'm just saying, I really want to do this. Adding your own child can't be that big a deal to Marques and Joel."

I'd meant it as a joke, but my mother's face went rigidly blank.

For a second, neither of them said anything. What had I said wrong?

"True." Daddy cleared his throat. "We can make it work, Nut."

Surprise flickered in Mommy's eyes. Daddy was the creative. She was the business brains. The Cee Oh Oh. He didn't go against her decisions too often. But keeping to some code they had established way before I arrived on the scene, she didn't strike him down a second time.

Daddy sat up straighter, playing strict. "No special

treatment, Marigold. Am I understood?" I nodded and he smiled. "Good. Welcome aboard."

I jumped up and hugged him around the neck.

"Thank you, Daddy."

"Thank Mommy, too," he whispered as he kissed my cheek.

My mother's jaw was clenched, but she accepted my hug and held on as I thanked her.

"Is this what you want, Mari?" she asked, low.

I nodded. She squeezed me hard, then released.

"Like Daddy said, no special treatment," she said tightly. Emotion flickered in her eyes, then was gone. "Be careful what you ask for, little Miss." She tapped my butt. "Go make sure your wardrobe has what it needs for a working summer."

I didn't have to be told twice.

CHAPTER .5.

I was so busy working to get myself into Style High that I'd almost forgotten Justice was mad at me. It hit fresh the next morning.

First days of summer are plump and juicy with possibility. Phones jumping with late-night texts and DMs on socials. So much chatter that the messages are blazing in your head while you sleep.

I rolled over and grabbed my phone, heart pit-pattering, hoping to see something in the sea of texts from Justice.

I had a storm of messages from Sammie and Rachel— one of them already counting the cheddar she'd make at work; the other, last-minute second-guessing life in the sticks; and my Buzz timeline was flooded with pics of last-day-of-school swim parties and beach nights that nobody had bothered to invite me to.

But nothing from Justice.

I jumped, startled when Ms. Sadie appeared at my door. I swear I don't know how she moves that quiet.

"Well, good morning." The sun through my window made her smiling cheeks glow. "I hope this mean you planning on coming to the church with me today."

I fake yawned. "I'm still tired."

Her hands went to her hips. "Too tired for the Lord?"

Like I could win that argument. I stayed mum.

She came over and sat on the edge of my bed.

"Your momma said you asked about being a part of the little program at the company." She patted my leg. "Good."

"I guess it's good. Mommy acted like she didn't want me to do it."

"You know your momma." A shadow crossed her face but was gone just as fast. "She thinking when she sleeping. That's just her way."

I pulled my knees to my chest, glancing down at my phone. Not that Justice would be up this early. For a second, I thought about going to Beth U with Ms. Sadie. She didn't let me use my phone at the church. I'd be too busy to obsess whether he'd call or not.

I hope he didn't think I was gonna text first. If anything, he owed me an apology.

I heard his name mentioned and caught the tail end as Ms. Sadie said, "Your daddy almost didn't give him this job ' cause he figure he like you or you like him." She nodded, confirming that my surprise was the appropriate reaction. "Me and your momma told him it wasn't fair to hold it against him. There's worse things in the world than people becoming close. And even though you too young to date, he a nice boy. I like him."

She put her chin up in defiance and looked like the world's oldest teenager.

I couldn't help smiling. I had no idea what I'd missed and why she was talking about Justice. I listened, hoping to catch up and not reveal I hadn't been paying one bit of attention.

"Maybe your momma worried about the same thing."

"That me and Justice are going to get close?" I asked, putting one and one together but getting three. I had no idea what she was talking about.

She frowned and I waited on her to fuss about hating to repeat herself. Instead she shook her head as she stood up. "What I'm saying is, both your momma and daddy have their own concerns about you growing up this summer."

Her voice broke. Her lips glued shut for a second, while she got herself together, and then she finished with her special kind of Ms. Sadie love—half annoyed, half mush. "But everybody gotta grow up, some time. It's just your turn."

I nodded like I understood. It satisfied her.

She wiped her hands across her dress, smoothing away invisible wrinkles, and stood tall as her tiny, barely five feet would get her.

"I guess I better get used to going off by myself this summer. I'mma miss you and Sammie." She blew me a kiss. "Go ahead and enjoy your time off till work start."

I blew a kiss back.

I didn't get how working at Flexx had anything to do with me growing up. It wasn't a real job. But I thought about her saying Justice almost didn't get into Style High. And I hurt for him. He seemed like he wanted it so bad. I wanted it to work for him.

I really did.

I'd never called him my best friend aloud. I couldn't. It would hurt Rachel's feelings and plus, I don't know what box he'd check, for me, on a friendship test.

That was funny. Like Justice would ever take a friendship test. I could hear him now saying, That's some Flo mess. I can't fade that.

A tiny pain shot through my stomach thinking about him saying I was like everybody else at school.

I turned my back on my phone. I wasn't calling him. Period. If he didn't call me, he'd just have to be surprised when I bust into Flexx big and bold, Monday morning.

I said a final goodbye to Rachel as she packed. I rearranged my Wall of Hall drawings by season. By noon, I had rearranged my entire room. The black-and-white ottoman that looked like the back of a spotted pony was now off to the side of the Wall—like a nice spot to sit in a museum to admire the exhibit; and I'd plumped up the pillows in my window seat.

I sat on the floor beneath it (now I didn't want to mess up the pillows), sketch book in my lap, mind weaving my next design. Lost in my own world.

Next thing I knew, I heard the clank and rattling of Ms. Sadie making dinner. My stomach growled in appreciation.

I was deep into sketching a romper when my phone rang. I accepted the call with my toe without looking to see who it was, figuring it was Rachel, ready to back out of going to Camp Boonies.

"Hello? If you scurred, say you scurred," I said as I searched around on all fours for my red pencil.

Justice's voice floated from the floor.

"Ayne, who you curbing like that?"

I froze, momentarily caught off guard. I eased back onto my butt, nudging the phone with my foot until I'd slid it close enough to pick up.

"Hello?" he asked.

"Hey," I said flatly, the hurt fresh.

He'd said I was like everybody else at school. He might as well have called me a sellout or worse, an Oreo, the stupid name Samej's friends called me the first time they met me. She bawled them out for it, and it had been fine ever since. It still stung.

"My bad, was you waiting on another call?" he asked, sounding like he'd seriously just let me go if I said yes.

I opened my mouth and exhaled silently toward the ceiling before answering.

"I just figured it was Rachel . . . since nobody else really been blowing up my phone, today."

My pride was rewarded with a faint chuckle from his side of the call.

"You could have called me, you know," he said.

"Why would I?" Anger rose in my throat. "Since I'm just riding your tip to Regents like everybody else at school, I figured I'd just wait to see who's gonna be in your place once you take your show to a new school next year."

The words, bitter and sarcastic, felt good. I knew he'd probably come back at me strong. And I had nothing. That was my best shot.

My hands trembled just a little as I found the red pencil under a sketch of a pair of palazzo pants. I let the drawing calm me, loving how the pants billowed, like air literally flowed inside.

It took a few seconds before I realized he was laughing on the other end.

"I deserved that," he said. "Put your dukes down, I didn't come to fight."

I ran the red pencil over the romper, shading more than it needed to keep myself from saying anything. He'd started this. I wanted him to finish it.

"I didn't mean to come for you like that, the other day," he said. "I was hot at the dean, not you."

I took the phone off speaker and held it up to my ear to catch every inflection in his voice, to confirm that our first fight, ugly and tense, was over.

"I know you're not like everybody else there. That was messed up of me, dogging you like that."

"Thanks . . . for apologizing," I said, feeling light enough to float.

"I was tripping, thinking the dean would be happy

that I'd gotten into a program like Style High." He sucked his teeth. "Man, he acted like he didn't even hear me. It set me off."

I eagerly co-signed. "That was foul on his part."

"You mad at me?" he asked, sounding genuinely curious.

I could almost see him wiping his thumb across his eyebrows, expecting the blow of me saying yes. It made me happy to think he was a little worried.

"No. But now, thanks to you, I'm working this summer," I said.

"Yo, wait, what? What that gotta do with me?"

I forced more poutiness. "Trying to prove to you I'm not bougie I hemmed myself up with a job."

He fell out laughing. "The fact that you got a job to prove you not bougie is bougie."

I protested weakly. "No, it's not."

"Mari, nobody gets a job to prove they not bougie except bougie people."

Glad we were back on the same page, I wanted to tell him how important what he thought about me was. How lonely I'd be if he transferred. I didn't because that would have been weird. Instead, I shot my announcement like it was a T-shirt in one of those cannon things they have at the basketball games.

"Well then, you really gonna think this is bougie because it's with Style High." Silence. I thought the call dropped. "Jus?" I looked at the phone, saw the call counter still ticking away. "Ju—"

"I'm still here," he said.

"Oh." I chuckled. "So yeah, I asked my parents if I could do it 'cause it sounds dope. I been getting my design game up. Even added four more designs to my wall."

"But you didn't even know about it till a few days ago," he said.

I sidestepped the gray cloud I heard in his voice.

"I mean I did technically. I was there when my parents created it." I didn't mean to ask for permission. Hello, it's my parents' company. But I couldn't take us arguing again. "Do you feel some kind of way about me doing Style High?"

My heart thumped hard in my chest. I kind of didn't want to hear the truth. Still, he answered so fast it felt like a lie.

"What? No, it don't matter to me." He did a weird thing, clearing his throat real loud like he needed it to say the rest. "Like you said, it's your people's company. So, yeah, cool."

It didn't feel cool. But pushing him would have only

made him deny it. Or worst, admit he really wasn't cool with it.

I didn't want to argue anymore. I let him play it off, pretending that I didn't hear how his voice felt higher. Phony. He peppered me with questions about how I ended up a part of Style High. Hipped me to the Style High hashtag the three of them had created to find each other on the Buzz.

"There's a hashtag?" I asked.

He boasted. "Yup. I started it, hoping the other trainees would find it and they did. We might even get that joint trending this summer."

Three people could get something trending? Well all righty, then.

I kept that to myself, glad that his joy wiped away the silence from before. "Y'all hyping it, huh?" I asked.

"You know it. Put something out there with it. They'll hit you back," he said.

And like that, the hesitation I heard (thought I heard?) was gone.

"Naw, I'm good," I said.

"I'mma let 'em know we working with the BD."

"If that means bosses' daughter I'mma need you to stop right now," I said, meaning it but keeping it light.

He laughed. "Even if it means bossy daughter?"

"Wow. Whatever, Jus. But for real, don't give them a heads-up, please."

"Heads-up?"

"I don't want them feeling some kind of way before they even know me." I hated the apology in my voice, but I didn't take it back.

"How they gonna feel some kind of way and don't know you?" he said.

"Okay, you don't know how girls do." I felt the tension rising and backed down. "So just don't . . . please."

"They both sway, but ay whatever. I won't say nothing," he said.

We talked on, him telling me everything he knew about the girls and me picking my words carefully so he wouldn't think I was being petty. At some point, he promised to add me to their group chat, if I wanted. I didn't. And I wasn't hearing things, he sounded kind of relieved when I told him not to.

Relieved.

How sway.

Except, not.

CHAT-TER

Mari_Golden:
You up? ●●

Got-Sammit:
Thank you for calling Burger
Haven may I take your order
please? 🍔

Mari_Golden:
😂 you tripping.

Got-Sammit:
I smell like grease and onion. A
dog chased me home thinking I
had food in my pocket.

Mari_Golden:
Wait, for real?

Got-Sammit:
lol not the dog part.

Mari_Golden:
lolls be real w/me please

Got-Sammit:
always

Mari_Golden:
do Mara and Shay still clown me behind
my back?

Got-Sammit:

Not to me. Deyknowbetta

Mari_Golden:

Do they be thinking I'm fake down?

Got-Sammit:

For real, who knows. Even if they
do it's just jealousy. People always
gon find something wrong w/
somebody who got stuff they
want

Mari_Golden:

I get so tired of it tho. Mags act like I
can get them an invite to the cookout.
Pressed to be down. But then in Marks
people be ready take my Black card
away if I say the wrong thing. Bruh, it's
so played out.

Got-Sammit:

What's up? Who I gotta roll up
on?

Mari_Golden:

😍 Thanks but nobody. Just getting
nervous about tomorrow.

Got-Sammit:

Your boy be there tho. He not gon
let nobody come for you.

Mari_Golden:

I guess

Got-Sammit:

🫣 Smoke?

Mari_Golden:

No. IDK. I'm tripping.

Got-Sammit:

You be alright, girl. Just be you.
And if a broad wanna trip, tell
Aunt Nut, she prolly still know
how knuck. 💪

Mari_Golden:

No doubt. 😄 It's good tho. Miss u.

Got-Sammit:

Miss u too. Why don't you and Jus
come through Saturday. I hook
y'all up.

Mari_Golden:

K

CHAPTER .6.

I awoke to Daddy's cologne drifting over my head and around my nose. The nutty sweetness mixed with his body chemistry made a scent that was uniquely him.

He shook me gently, whispering.

"Mari."

I winked one eye open at my phone.

6:00 a.m.

And he was already dressed and ready to roll.

"Want to ride into work with me?"

There was a laugh in the question. Still, my hair bonnet made a schwep schewp sound as I shook my head vigorously against my pillow. I reached my arms up, like a baby, and he lowered himself for me to hug. He released me and stood over the bed, ready to chat now that I was fully awake.

"It means a lot to me that you want to work at Flexx this summer."

The gold flecks in his eyes brightened. They only did that when he was emotional about something—happy, sad, mad, excited—like little fairies that danced in his eyes to confirm what was on his heart.

My smile was crooked as I tried not to blow my stank morning breath in his face.

"I guess you know your mother has some reservations."

Schwep schwep as I nodded agreement.

"I don't come between you and your mom too often . . . I'm sure you noticed."

Notice when it stopped me from getting my way, I felt like saying, but settled for a shrug.

"Me and her see this differently." He stared down at me, intently. "I think you need to live in the world outside of Flowered. I think Nut would be okay with us just telling you what that world is like . . . how it was for us. Flowered will make you well-rounded, academically. But the way you and those kids live, thinking everything can be solved by your parents' money . . ." He frowned. "Only me and your mother can help shatter that myth. And putting yourself in different circles is a good way to do that."

He smiled down at me, eager for me to jump aboard his train.

I think my father must have been a street preacher in a previous life. He had a way of making things make sense even if you started out not agreeing with him. My adrenaline pumped, scared and excited for the day ahead.

He reached down and chucked my chin.

"This will be a summer you'll never forget, Marigold. The chance to impact fashion changed my life and I think it'll do the same for you." He smiled tenderly. "All the better that you'll get to experience it right here in DC beside kids your age who wouldn't normally have this chance. You'll really get to see what Flexx is all about. And I think you'll understand why me and your mom put so much time into it."

There was a pause, pregnant with something else.

I waited, trying to blow out my breath sideways so it wasn't going up to his face.

He shook himself out of some thought.

"One last thing. This is between me and you but . . . I nearly denied Justice a spot in the program."

I pulled the sheet up to my mouth to block my heated breath and feigned shock.

"Daddy, why?"

"Justice would be all right with or without Style High. Flowereds will use his skill and then ship him off to a good college to play basketball." His lips were thin and disapproving. "The boy has the brains. It'll be on him to use them."

"Well, I'm glad you picked him," I muttered through the sheets. "The dean wasn't happy about him not doing summer league this year."

His eyes tried and failed to hide their surprise.

"Not happy?"

I turned my head away slightly, hoping I was blowing downwind. I told him what the dean had said to Justice.

The flecks in daddy's eyes grew lighter as his frown deepened.

"It figures." He folded his arms. "Flowereds is into that plantation mentality. Nothing free is ever free, Marigold. They gave him a scholarship so now they own him until graduation. Well, good for Justice for stepping out on his own."

"Daddy, you flip-flopping like a mug." I giggled. "First, he's fine on his own. Now you're his cheering section."

"Look, I didn't have all the information, at first. Always reserve the right to change your opinion once you find out all the information. Hear me?" He raised an eyebrow at me until I nodded agreement, then cracked a smile. "Second of all, you were almost there."

His fingers were inches apart.

"Almost where?" I asked, eyebrows furrowed.

"Almost to the finish line without blowing your stinky breath on me till I got you talking about old Yes Sir."

I defended myself, purposely blowing my dragon breath his way.

"Nobody told you to pick o' dark thirty as the time to have a father-daughter heart-to-heart."

He waved his hand, pretending to shoo my morning stank away, laughing as he headed to the door.

"All right, baby girl. I'm glad we talked."

"Wait." I sat up. "So why did you end up giving Justice the position?"

If Justice knew how close he'd come to not making Style High, he'd be crushed. Anxiety butterflies fluttered in my gut.

Daddy peered at me from the door, like he was weighing what to say. It was the first time that talk about work didn't flow from him like a babbling brook. Then whatever debate he was having with himself ended.

"I liked his answers about the future of hip-hop style,"

he said. "And his portfolio was impressive. He has the knack."

I exhaled, relieved. Thank God Justice was one of those people good at whatever he wanted.

"Thank you," I hollered before Daddy slipped out the door.

He turned around. "What for?"

I opened my mouth to say the real reason—for giving Justice a chance—then stopped.

"For giving me something to do this summer. Don't tell Mommy or Ms. Sadie, though, or they'll OD on planning my life," I said.

He chuckled knowingly.

"You got that, baby girl. You won't regret it," he said with a wink before closing the door behind him.

Daddy's little speech got me moving. I'd already picked my outfit, a black cropped top with big pink roses that hugged my body but didn't show too much belly, and a chiffon high-low skirt. The high front of the skirt gave my short legs length and I added to the illusion by pairing it with my black heel booties. The shoes weren't the best for standing in too long, but it was an L I was going to have to take.

For the sake of fashion, I grabbed my black bowler hat as a last-minute touch. I sat it as far back on my head as I could without it falling off. It made me feel artsy—the one thing I rarely claimed, but it felt right.

As soon as Ms. Sadie saw me, she scowled. "Those work clothes?"

"For Flexx, yes," I said, grabbing the carafe of orange juice and pouring a swallow.

"Everybody gonna be dressed showing their stomach so it make it all right for you?" she asked, hands on her hips.

I downed the orange juice, stuffed a piece of bacon into my mouth, and smushed my greasy lips against her cheeks.

"Thank you, Ms. Sadie, I will try and have a good day."

She hugged me tight before I could pull away. "All right, I don't want to start your morning off wrong." She patted my back and shuffled over to the sink, her voice choked. "Sometimes it just seem like you growing up too fast. But at least none of your goodies showing."

"You taught me better than that," I said, with an innocent grin.

She hmphed but wouldn't turn around, which meant she was crying.

She was a tough old lady with the world's softest heart. Just to make her happy I grabbed another piece of bacon and was gone.

There were at least a dozen mothers out pushing strollers. Some of them had a toddler or two up front and a baby in the back. I recognized a few of the regular morning striders who were out when I headed to school. They waved, smiled, or nodded. I waved back but kept my stride strong and fast-paced. T-Hill was a hot spot for people who wanted to live in the city but not feel like they did. It had turned into Baby Central like it was something in the water.

I sidestepped an oncoming jog stroller and rounded the bend to the red line. Down 41st Street, swatches of green trees in front of brick town homes gave way to penthouse-style condos. I went from dodging baby buggies to bumping shoulders with pinstriped men and women on their way someplace important.

At Albermarle Street, the traffic was shoulder to shoulder, everybody doing the rush hour waltz—long, hurried steps, head high, eyes forward. I merged with the herd toward the escalator.

I kept to the right—the slow lane. Most everybody else galloped their way down the left side. Futile. We'd all make the same train anyway.

I was only going to be on the Metro for two stops. I could have walked. I wanted more time to sit and think before I stepped into the office. It was my last chance to get my game face on.

I closed my eyes and listened to the sounds of the Metro, waiting for the conductor to announce my point of no return, "K Street Business District."

On the three-block walk from the station to Flexx's tall, all-glass fifteen-story building, I kept thinking I was going to push through the revolving doors and fall into some kind of rabbit hole. Like something had suddenly changed because I was working there instead of only stopping in for a visit.

I hustled through the doors into the cavernous lobby shoulder to shoulder with other Flexx staffers. They shot off like a cannon spit them out. Everyone stepped with purpose and flashed their plastic picture badges to Mr. Clyde, the security guard. He nodded or tipped his hat with barely a glance at the credentials, silently waving mostly everybody through to the elevators. Those he didn't had forgotten their badges, forcing him to check licenses and give stern looks of disapproval as he nodded them through stiffly, mad that they'd made him do more work.

I walked like I was trying to avoid land mines.

I slid the badge that my parents made me update every September out of my bag, placed the lanyard around my neck, and followed the flock. Through the clacking of people's heels on the floor and murmurs of morning conversation, the sound of my name being called floated and got trapped somewhere on its way up into the high ceiling. Somehow, I still heard it.

I turned toward where I thought it came from.

Justice and two girls stood off to the left of the steel U-shaped reception desk—the area where visitors without badges were forced to seek permission to enter behind the velvet rope. Two women, both with their hair pulled back in identical French twists and wearing beige button-down shirts with the blue Flexx logo above the right breast, stood behind the desk talking.

The older woman was Ms. Sarah. She'd been a lobby host forever. She was probably some kind of supervisor by now, but she still did the same thing she always did—made sure anybody requesting a badge deserved a badge. She recognized me, smiled, and waved, but seeing I required no work on her part, went back to her conversation.

I waved back, then made my way over. When I finally reached the group, they opened the huddle enough for me to stand in the gap, but no one said anything, not even Justice.

I gripped the handle of my bag with both hands and smiled way too hard.

"Hey," I sang, then added, "Justice."

"Hey," Justice said, distracted. "They won't let us in." He introduced me, hurriedly. "My bad. Marigold, this is Chandra and Kara."

"You can just call me Mari," I said to their muttered hellos.

We all pretended not to check one another out, while totally doing it—eye contact, glance away, eye contact, glance away.

Chandra was a tiny little thing. She was so skinny I don't think even the ten pounds cameras supposedly added would do much. Long brown microbraids streaked with blonde were piled high in a wiggly bun. A few braids that managed to escape tickled her shoulder, bare in a strapless beige maxi dress with navy blue stripes going all around. If the stripes were doing their job, they were giving her a couple pounds. Which meant she was truly tiny.

Kara was about five feet tall. She wore purple-and-black high-waisted shorts, a black tank top, and a sequined shrug that shimmered. She had a cute face, round and pie-shaped with a small nose to match. She stood, arms crossed, legs slightly apart, looking from me, to Justice, back to the reception desk without blinking away whenever I met her gaze.

Right as our silence slid to awkward, Chandra broke the ice.

"Oh my God. This so wild. Isn't this nuts? You're Marigold Johnson, right?" she blurted, words streaming a mile a minute. I'd barely nodded before she looked at Justice and Kara for more confirmation. They let her go on without responding. "To be here is off-the-charts nuts. But Marigold in the program too . . . that's like, it makes it so legit."

Kara's head shook slow side to side. It felt like disapproval.

Chandra felt it too. She frowned, then just as fast her right eyebrow shot up and her hand went to her hip. "What? Y'all can sit here and act like it's no big deal, but it is." Her bun bobbled as she talked on and on. It sort of hurt my head hearing her words shoot like bullets, but she was hyping me up, so I stayed quiet. "Mr. and Mrs. Johnson could have put Marigold in any kind of enrichment program they wanted. Some super secret kind on some Illuminati stuff. But they have her here with us. Kicking it regular people style."

Justice snickered. "Not regular people though. You not regular, Mari?"

He said it like a joke, but there was something underneath I didn't like.

Then Kara jumped in, eyebrows frowning at Chandra. "You acting like her people God or something. They like everybody else."

She hadn't said my parents stank or were serial killers. She hadn't said nothing bad at all. Still, there was a challenge in her gaze.

A familiar heaviness sat in my stomach. It was my first day of sixth grade, again, when circles shifted and I hoped one of them would pick me. Hoped Rachel wouldn't suddenly realize she belonged with the other Legs and not "the Black girl."

It was the exact same sick feeling.

I forced myself to keep eye contact and answered calmly, "Facts. They are."

Then, like that, Kara changed up. A real smile reached her eyes. Her cute face was almost pretty. "Then again, who knows. Maybe her father is part of the Illuminati." The smile she turned to me was the kind you drew on a picture—

straight, no teeth. "Wink once if he is, Marigold . . . I mean Mari."

Chandra stared at me, mouth open, like she really believed my father was part of some secret society. I played along.

"How you know this program not the first step to getting there yourself?"

My eyebrow hovered in a soft curve. I prayed she'd take it as the joke I meant it.

She snorted softly and looked around the crowded lobby. "Shoot, we can't even get past the French Twist Sisters. So, I doubt it."

"Big facts," Justice said. His black tee shirt gripped the bulge of his toned biceps. "Mari, you need use your connect to get us past Ol' Otis the security guard."

His head jerked toward Mr. Clyde and everyone bust out laughing, just another note in the morning's symphony.

Mr. Clyde was a former bouncer and was more fit than he looked under his gray-and-blue uniform.

"I don't think you want none of him," I said, wanting to add, Say please, but was scared it would come off wrong. "Y'all don't have badges?"

It was a silly question and Kara didn't waste a second pointing it out.

"Real talk, if we did we wouldn't need the connect."

Chandra co-signed. "Our packets didn't say anything about badges. I just assumed they'd let us up." She nodded toward Ms. Sara. "But that lady said somebody from upstairs would have to escort us up. Justice was the one who suggested we wait for you before we called anybody."

Justice's eyes crinkled at the ends, uncertain. An apology, maybe, for outing me.

"Should we call upstairs or can you get us through?" he asked.

"I can at least try," I said, not wanting to sound cocky even though I knew Ms. Sarah would let me have my way. "Wait here."

I felt all of their eyes on me as I walked over to the reception desk. I fought the urge to check myself for flaws—wedgies, wrinkles, or flyaway hair—and smiled big when Ms. Sara greeted me. We talked a few seconds about me working there and the merits of working young, then I explained about the trainees.

She looked everyone over once, then yelled to Mr. Clyde over the morning din.

"Clyde, these kids are going up with Marigold. They in that new program."

I waved, shining a beauty pageant smile. "Hi, Mr. Clyde."

"Hey, Mari." He raised his hand and gave the trainees a curt command to come over.

He wanded Justice with the gray stick that looked like a hand vacuum without the sucky part and motioned for Chandra and Kara to open their bags. Then we were through.

Chandra thanked me five times before the elevator door opened to our floor.

It was OD, but more than I got from Justice or Kara.

I tried not to care.

CHAPTER .7.

Determined to show everything was sway, I dove right in as we walked to the conference room.

"So, where is everybody from?" I put my hand up at Justice, playfully. "Bemp, not you."

He smushed me back. "Bemp. Marks Park all day." He stood three fingers on his shoulder in a M. The Marks salute.

Kara laughed a little too hard.

In the few seconds before she answered, I checked her out again and silently answered the question for myself.

Holly Heights.

She had three holes in her ear; oversized hoop earrings in the main hole and ruby studs in the other two. Her hair was long, black, silky extensions in a side ponytail that swayed gently over her right shoulder. I was sure I saw the slight glimmer of a tongue ring, though she must have had it for a while because she knew how to talk around it without sounding like she had a lisp. She had rings on nearly every finger, two on some, and this mini-egg–sized silver ball ring on her ring finger.

It wasn't bad, just too much. Holly Heights girls always overdid it.

She smiled wide, cocking her head as she announced, "Holly Heights. Meow." The side pony brushed her elbow. It was a decent weave. Too much, but decent.

I felt Justice grin before I saw it. "Yeah, Kara know my boy, Mook."

"With his crazy self," she said.

Her and Justice laughed. I had no idea who Mook was. But of course, she'd know someone he knew. I pounded the jealousy out through my feet, picking up the pace to the conference room.

I almost forgot Chandra hadn't said anything, until she spoke up, demurely.

"Rolling Park representing."

"Almost all the hoods in the house," Kara said with approval.

"All except Brandy Heights," Justice said, his long stride easing to walk beside Kara.

"And what about you, Mari? You're a Hill chick, right?" Chandra asked as she pulled up beside me.

She bowed her head in mock reverence and smiled at me.

Totten Hill was two blocks' worth of houses. They sat on a high round of land overlooking the downtown. Drive through and they looked like any other city block of brick-faced town homes. But they were some of District City's most expensive places to live and sometimes it was hard to tell what was true and what was rumor. One place had an underground pool . . . in a townhouse. True. Someone had built a mini Ferris wheel in their basement. False. Either way, trying to outdo your neighbor was a sport on T-Hill. The winner was whoever got their house featured in stuff like *House Gorgeous* or *Crazy Cribs*. People treated T-Hill like it was a far-off place.

I'm sure Chandra wanted me to acknowledge the proper amount of respect she put on my nabe, but I hit her with the "umhm" and kept it pushing.

We reached the frosted orange glass door of the conference room. I could just make out the shape of two people somewhere behind the door—Marques and Joel— and was about to open it when Kara said, "That's right. Not all of us from the hood. Must be nice."

Only Mommy's words hitting me over the head, reminding me how important this experience was for them, kept my tongue in check.

"Come on, y'all, we're all Team Style High this summer," Chandra said, voice tense with fake cheer. She reached over to touch Kara's shoulder. "No matter where we're from."

Kara shifted away just enough so Chandra's fingers hung in midair. "It always matters where you from."

The hurt look on Chandra's face pushed me to her defense. I looked Kara in her eye and said, "Even if it matters, you have to put it aside while we're here."

Her head reared back and her eyes widened. Before I could give myself a point for shutting her down, she snorted. "Spoken like the boss's daughter."

I was jerked forward as the door was pulled open.

"You good," Justice asked.

I heard the laugh in his voice and scolded the hurt feelings flaring, making my neck hot. How many times had one of us stumbled over our feet and we laughed as we asked, "You all right?" Why was I tripping this time?

I let go of the door, slinking past Marques as he looked on disapproving.

"Nice of everyone to join us," he said. "Y'all are late."

I almost apologized. But it wasn't my fault they hadn't gotten past security without me.

Marques quickly placed himself at the front of the conference room, fussing with his old school poofy pompadour hairstyle. His style partner, Joel, was already at the head of the table, his long, relaxed hair pulled back in a bun held in with colorful plastic sticks. His big apple cheeks plumped as he smiled at us.

Seeing Joel relaxed me.

"Come on in, kids," he said, even though we were already in.

Marques jumped in, staking his claim as "the boss." He swept his hand at the multitude of chairs surrounding the big table. "Have a seat."

I sat in the chair nearest the door. Justice sat beside me. I couldn't help thinking—Oh now you want roll with me?

Kara sat beside him, Chandra by her.

We were a good half a football field away, prompting Marques to speak louder but not come closer. When he talked, he pronounced every word like he was reading a teleprompter. As he went on making his unfunny jokes,

"I'm Marques Hilton . . . no relation to Paris," I leaned into Justice and low-talked. He leaned his head just enough to hear but not look like he wasn't paying attention.

"Hey, Sammie want us to stop by Burger Haven, Saturday. You in?"

He nodded twice slow.

"Cool."

"Did you want the floor, Marigold?" Marques asked, his sleek eyebrow arched.

"Caught," I heard someone mutter. Pretty sure it was Kara.

"I didn't say anything," I said. I clasped my hands on top of the table to show how good of a student I was being. Marques folded his skinny arms and put us in our places, reminding us that he and Joel were our advisors.

Not chaperones.

Not tour guides.

Not babysitters.

Well, all right then.

Suddenly, syrup poured from his mouth. "Now, we have two very special guests who would like to say hello."

My parents came in through a side panel in the wall that was only visible once it was opened.

Mommy was a breath of fresh air after Marques's

military-style greeting. She looked very Cee Oh Oh-ish in a black linen sleeveless shift and black peekaboo heels. A silver and opal link chain necklace hung in loops around her neck, glistening. "If you don't know, I'm Manita Johnson." Her smile hid that she was the bad cop to my dad's good most times. "I'm cofounder and Chief Operating Officer here at Flexx Unlimited." Unlike Marques, she stood at the side of the table, right across from where we all sat. Her nails clicked softly as she leaned forward and rested her hands on the tabletop. "You all can call me Ms. Manita or Mrs. Johnson. Welcome to Style High."

Joel and Marques clapped, enthusiastically but polite, like they were afraid to bring their hands all the way together. My father joined in with a slow, booming clap.

Mommy's voice lilted, going up and down melodically as she did what my parents did best: made everyone feel like they owned a piece of Flexx. When she stepped away, finished, we clapped.

Justice whispered, "I love your moms, man."

I couldn't help grinning. Not like I had anything to do with it, but I loved that Flexx was making him happy after the dean showed his tail.

Right on cue, my father took Mommy's place at the side

of the table. In his camel-colored cargo pants and yellow argyle sweater vest, he was an older, polished version of the interns that Flexx kept in abundance. If it weren't for a few grays in his well-trimmed beard, he could have easily been mistaken for one of the less senior staffers.

"After going over your applications and through your portfolios, I feel like I already know each of you. And some of you, I do." His eyes stopped on Justice for a few seconds before sweeping back and forth down the line, the energetic kid to my mother's steady teacher's gaze. "Welcome to the family."

Justice sat up straighter, practically beaming light at being called out.

I was going to have a good time teasing him later about his stan-dom.

Kara made a sound like hmmph or mmph. I leaned back in my chair, pretending to stretch, so I could stare slyly a few more seconds. She looked bored. I'd never seen anybody Daddy couldn't win over and doubted she'd be the first.

Daddy built the trainee program up, dropping the word *future* a couple times. No wonder people felt like they owned Flexx. He made it feel like a private club and they (we?) had just become members. He gave Marques and Joel a tiny salute, said that we were learning from the best. Marques's teeny frame seemed to swell at the compliment.

I sneaked another peek down the line. Chandra's eyes were big and glazed, like she was afraid to blink. Justice was listening and he looked calm, but his leg was jiggling a hundred miles an hour again. I slid my hand off the table and placed it on his knee, trying to send him chill vibes. He snatched away, like my hand had burned him. For a second our eyes met. His seemed to apologize before giving his full attention back to Daddy.

Daddy turned it on good for us, too. When he talked about our future at Flexx, I felt Justice and Chandra sit up at attention. Kara's chin stayed propped on her hand. She seemed like she was miles away. I wasn't getting future of hip-hop from her at all.

By the time Daddy ended his speech with "I need three things from you this summer. Do well. Open doors. Get paid," Chandra and Justice didn't need any prompting from Marques to clap. Kara joined in with the fake clap, where your hands make the motion but not the noise.

With my phone in my lap, I slyly texted Justice:

Kara hit us w/da phony clap 😂

I thought he'd laugh, smile, or hit me back with something—a joke between us.

He looked down at his phone, squinted, then put his phone into his back pocket.

Woomp woomp.

CHAPTER .8.

Throughout the morning, every time I was tempted to text Justice to joke about:

—how Marques's pompadour hairstyle made him look like an out-of-work musician from another decade;

—how Chandra loved calling my name like she was winning points for it;

—how I was already looking forward to me, him, and Sammie chilling on Saturday;

then I'd remember he'd igged my earlier message and resist.

I endured the Flexx story—the entire story—with my fingers burning to share my misery with Sammie, Rachel, shoot, maybe even Ms. Sadie, except she didn't have a cell phone. It didn't matter, I didn't have a chance to pull my phone out without risking getting caught.

Just when I thought we were going to be stuck in the conference room again, Joel, the Style High God of Mercy, smiled upon us.

"Your paperwork is done. You have badges. And you now know from whence you came. You're officially, official." He bowed deeply. "So now, to the Closet."

Finally.

I popped out of the chair so fast, Chandra giggled.

"Dang, Mari. You a track chick? If not, you should be."

I was. Everybody at Flo-A had to do a sport because, according to the Board Of Trustees, an active body feeds an active mind. I didn't answer her, though. I didn't need to. Chandra liked to talk and was already asking, "Why we working in a closet?"

I could have answered her. But the Closet had to be experienced. It's a candy shop for fashion addicts. A tricked-out department store hidden inside of an office building.

Joel, with Marques bringing up the rear, led us to the elevator, reminiscing about his days as a young style protégé. He made grand gestures with his arms as he talked. When the elevator door opened, he stepped out, bowed, and whispered dramatically, "Welcome to the Closet, young Style Heads."

Floor-to-ceiling shoe racks ran along the walls. Six open styling areas—hubs—were decked out with enough mirrors so you couldn't miss an angle, each with a tiny round riser in the middle so clients could show off their new style.

In front of each hub were a pair of Skittles-colored love seats, for the viewers of any spontaneous showing. Every few feet were tall custom-made bureaus with drawers specially made to hold jewelry, belts, and ties. And mannequins, mannequins everywhere. Not posed and primping, but headless, faceless mannies whose sole purpose was to be draped with outfits for review, then stripped naked again until the next time.

Some mannies kept silent vigil in the style hubs. Others were lined up in little cubbies, waiting their turn to be rolled out and put to work.

Five circles of racks, fat with clothes, played ring-around-the-rosy down the center of the entire floor. Evening dresses, shirts and blouses, slacks, shorts, skirts, and dresses mingled on the racks. Samples. A tease as to what was in store for lucky makeover victims. The real mother lode of clothes was deep down a hall in a warehouse-sized storeroom.

Officially it was the fashion library. Everyone simply called it "the Closet."

If you could enter and keep a straight face, then fashion wasn't in your blood.

I waited to see how the others would react.

"Oh my God," Chandra exclaimed. Her head swiveled from one thing to the next, trying to take it all in.

Kara looked from the style hubs to the wall-to-wall shoe racks like maybe she wanted to get closer. Touch to see if it was real. So, maybe she did have some fashion in her.

Justice's eyes were huge and his mouth open. He looked from one part of the room to another. His eyes lingered before moving on, like he wanted to make sure he was seeing what he saw.

Marques and Joel walked us through the flurry of activity, pointing out highlights. The summer interns, college students, had already made the Closet their home. The room was alive. Music played overhead, proving even more why it wasn't much of a library.

Two people sat on the purple love seat in the first styling hub, their heads together over something. Someone popped out of the fitting room to their right and they both jumped like a pit crew and began adjusting clothes, hands roaming frantically over the person from head to toe.

I edged up to Justice's side. "It's clutch, huh?"

I felt stupidly proud, a tour guide on a trip to a hidden world.

"Very," Justice answered.

Marques stopped in front of a styling area with an orange love seat. There were glossy black drafting desks and a small round table with four chairs behind the love seat. There was a small stack of white binders on the table. Our own mini conference area. Several mannies stood silently in front of the love seat at the ready to be draped in our creations.

I was anxious to put fabric to mannequin.

"Come on now, pick out your workstation," Marques said, feigning impatience. But even his sculpted brows seemed to relax a little as he observed our awe.

I hung out on the edge, letting the others pick first, Mommy's "ruining their experience" comment forever ringing in my ear.

Justice took one of the desks on the end.

Kara snagged the desk next to him, lazily pulling the chair out and sliding into it.

"Where you wanna sit, Mari?" Chandra asked.

I glanced over at Justice picking through the colored

pencils and other goodies in the desk's little cubby. A knot, stupid and hot, swelled in my throat. Had I expected him to hit the old elementary school I-saved-you-a-seat move? Throw his long leg over the desk's seat so Kara couldn't have sat there?

For real, I had.

"I'll take the end desk," I said, with cheer I didn't really mean.

"Okay. Cool." She wedged herself in at the desk between me and Kara.

"Don't get too comfortable," Joel announced. His stomach heaved as he tried to catch his breath and lecture at the same time. "It'll probably be a minute before you all sit here."

Our expressions of shared confusion brought a look of pleasure to Marques's face.

"All right, let's deal with the obvious," he said. A well-manicured nail slowly scaled down his cheek before curling under his chin. "I . . . well, me and Joel, have known Mari since she was eight years old. Watched her grow up. It is what it is." His right eyebrow flicked so hard, I thought it was going to rip from his face and come flying at us before boomeranging back onto his forehead. "All of you, Mari included, are on my turf now. Little sponges wanting to soak up my knowledge and the experience I've worked hard for." He paused, like he was waiting for us to argue, then carried on.

"I'm not cutting anybody a break. Y'all might only be thirteen?" His eyes rolled up, then he waved his hand like it didn't matter. "Or fourteen. Whichever. But every one of you probably have dreams of being me. I'm gonna make you work for that." He walked over and knocked twice on my desk. "Even Miss Mari."

"Ouch," Justice said under his breath, but loud enough for me to hear at my end of our tiny desk line.

Joel blew me a tiny kiss.

I smiled at him, happy somebody loved me.

Marques caught the exchange. Lips pressed together tight, he gave me and Joel a disapproving head shake. We were blowing his drill-sergeant vibe.

"Are we clear that this is not a game?" Marques asked.

The crew muttered their consent.

He glared at me. "Mari?"

"Yes, sir," I said, barely keeping my face straight.

I was sure he wanted to smile. He turned his back, supposedly to pick up his tablet from the love seat. When he faced us again the smile was ghost.

He flipped the tablet cover open.

"Let's work, then. What's the difference between a shell, blouse, chemise, and shirt?"

The background noise grew louder in the absence of anyone answering.

I kept my face blank, like I didn't know either. So, of course, Marques called me out.

"Mari, don't play stupid. Your little friends—" He took a breath. "I mean, your fellow trainees need to deal with the fact that you probably know more about the industry than some grown folk. It's gonna be a long summer if you dumb yourself down."

"Use your knowledge to help them." Joel stood in the very center of our hub, addressing me personally. "The sooner you all know the lingo, the sooner you'll get to do style work on clients."

At the mention of clients, Chandra raised her hand.

Marques bowed his head at her.

"I think it's a trick question because they're all the same thing. . . ." She squinched her lips to the left, thought for a second, then added, "Well, at least a chemise and shirt are."

The closest thing to a smile appeared on Marques's face. Joel clapped.

"But a shell is different," I said. "A shell doesn't have

a collar or buttons. A blouse could be the same thing as a chemise, though."

"Well, good, some of y'all came to play," Marques said.

Kara grunted. If Marques heard, he didn't say anything.

He shot off questions left and right, going from clothing styles to designers, what lines they produced, and even asking the year certain lines launched. I paused, every time, giving other people time to answer. Eventually, the air was electric as everybody, even Kara, shot their hand up to prove they knew a little something even if they didn't know a lot of everything.

At some point, Joel started tossing candy for correct answers.

As the game sped forward, it got rowdy when Justice was one point ahead of me and Chandra taunted, "Girls against the boy!" So Marques shut it down. His cover came over the tablet screen with a tiny thwap, subduing us. Talking smack was replaced by the sounds of candy chomping.

"There's hope, here," Marques said. "You still have a long way to go, but there's hope."

There was a tiny tug at the top of his lip. The closest he came to smiling.

His long, thin arm stretched out, fingers pointing. "In the cubby of your desks is a list of daily chores." He waited for everyone to pull out the paper. "Review it. Now's the time for questions if you don't understand any of the tasks outlined on it."

He stood, arms folded. Joel smoothed barely-there wisps at the back of his hair, waiting.

There were four jobs and a basic description of each on the paper:

Steamer

Accessory Inventory

Shoe Inventory

Runner

I read the page over and over, looking for the rest of the jobs: Stylist, or even Jr. Stylist and Client Interviewer.

I turned the page over. Blank.

Kara raised her hand. "It keeps saying to put stuff in 'inventory.' Isn't all this inventory?" She gestured to the racks and drawers throughout the space.

"Not even half of it," Joel said with a devilish grin. "But we won't overload you. Tomorrow, Ms. Tonya will give you all an orientation on our cataloging system and how to check out inventory. Then you'll head to the storeroom. That's where all the inventory is." He clapped between the words. "Every. Item."

Marques pointed to the small stack of binders at our

conference table. "Come grab one. All you ever want to know about Flexx and the detailed descriptions of your job roles are there."

We each slid a binder off the table. It was thick with papers divided into sections by a rainbow of colored tabs.

Chandra thumbed through hers as Marques continued.

"I suggest taking notes as you read. There might be a quiz."

Kara frowned and said exactly what I was thinking, "A quiz?"

"I think you already know I'm not about repeating myself," Marques said with an eyebrow raise.

I worked to keep my face neutral. They expected us to sit here in the middle of all these clothes and read a binder? I was blown and so was everybody else, based on how deflated they looked.

Justice raised his hand. I thought he was going to negotiate or question our new history lesson and I was ready to back him. But he only asked, "Do we get a lunch?"

"Of course," Joel said before Marques could answer. "Thirty minutes. Plenty of food trucks line up outside the building." He looked at his phone. "Probably there now. But don't sleep on this assignment. We're not going to teach you all how to steam or explain where things go. The binders give exact instructions that we expect you to commit to memory. Use the time wisely this afternoon."

"Excuse me, Mr. Joel—" Chandra started.

"Just Joel," he said with a smile.

Chandra beamed back. "Joel, um . . ." She pointed to a page. "Is this assignment due tomorrow?"

"By the end of the day, actually," Joel said. "Once you finish it, you can leave."

Kara peeped the page Chandra was on and flipped until she reached it. Her lips moved as she read over the directions. I reluctantly flipped to the page, afraid of what I'd find there. I breathed a silent sigh of relief when I saw it:

List three celebrities that helped propel Flexx's success.

What does fashion mean to you?

It could have been much worse. Kara didn't agree.

"How are we supposed to know the answer to this?" she asked, scowling.

"By reading through the material," Joel said patiently.

Kara squinted at the thick book. "The entire binder?"

"Read the instructions, Kara. It's not as bad as you think," Joel said.

Marques folded his arms, not bothering to coddle us.

"You have to crawl before you walk. Be thankful we took the time to put how to take those first steps in writing. Welcome to Flexx, young bucks. See you bright and early tomorrow."

He turned on his heel and walked off, dismissing us with his back.

Our section of the busy room was silent until Justice blew a raspberry. "Welp . . . chapter one . . ." His binder was open to the first page. He ran his finger over the words, like he was reading.

I played along. "Once upon a time in a land far away . . ."

Chandra eagerly joined in. "Two fashion moguls came to play."

"Nice," Justice said, grinning.

Kara pushed her binder away. "Sorry, I'm not with this. It's like being at school."

Chandra glanced my way, must have felt that I wasn't going to say anything, and spoke up. "It's not what I thought we'd be doing, but it's hardly like school." She looked over her shoulder to the activity behind us. "I mean, look. It's still really cool to be here." She shrugged. "I mean, speaking for myself."

"Nah, I'm with you," Justice said. "And if we work

together, we can get the answers to the first part of the assignment faster. Who down to do that?"

Chandra's hand shot up. Justice looked down the line at me.

Before I could answer, Kara scoffed. "Don't she already know the answers?"

She? Full-on irritation made my ears prickly with heat.

"I mean, all the better for us if she does, right?" Chandra asked, waiting on me to confirm.

"She has a name," I said, calmly.

Chandra stuttered. "Oh . . . oh, sorry. Marigold. Just saying—"

I held the bite in my voice back. "I get it." I finally answered Justice. "I can help with the history part. But we all have to study the job descriptions. I definitely wouldn't put it past Marques to give us a quiz on that kind of stuff."

Justice leafed through the binder. "Okay. Everybody pick a job and learn exactly how it's done . . . then we'll trade off information. I'll learn steamer."

I nodded and was about to select a position, then decided to play nice. "Kara, which role you want?"

She frowned. "I never said I was gonna do it."

Chandra cleared her throat. "I'll learn about being a runner."

"Just take shoe or accessory inventory, Kara. They seem kind of self-explanatory anyway," Justice suggested, calm like Kara hadn't already rejected the plan.

Amazingly she sucked her teeth and said, "Fine. Shoes, then."

She turned to the section in a huff. I tried to give Justice a "Really?" look, but his head was already buried in the binder.

Wow. Welcome to Flexx, indeed.

CHAPTER .9.

Mari_Golden:

Bruh, I hate it herrrre.

Got-Sammit:

Unah, don't even. No way what
you doing worse than flipping
burgers.

Mari_Golden:

You work at the register tho

Got-Sammit:

😕 Wow. Why you gotta always
win? LOL what up? How was it?

Sammie was only playing about not wanting me to

complain. But since she said it, I didn't want to be all dramatic about how the day had felt like one long history class, or how until he needed me to come to the rescue, it felt like Justice had carried me.

Maybe I was being sensitive.

The truth was, we had gotten through the assignment in only a few hours once we worked together. Still, Justice stayed busy keeping Kara on track. Every time she lapsed into complaining, he'd make jokes or enlist me and Chandra to help find the answers Kara could never find on her own.

And even though the question about what fashion meant to you wasn't something we could help each other with, he insisted that we all stay until all of us had finished the assignment. "Marques and Joel might be looking. It won't look right if we leave one of us here still working," he'd said, and Chandra readily agreed.

That tacked an extra twenty minutes onto the day while Kara struggled.

Like, girl, you applied for a whole style
trainee program, how do you not know
how to answer that?

I had texted to Justice, thinking he'd hit me back with an LOL or something.

Instead, he totally curbed me by looking at his phone

and not responding. Again. He only gave me some weak smile and shrugged.

Seriously?

It was like he didn't want to talk while we were at work. Like I was distracting him.

From what? Eighty pages of Flexx history and a twenty-step lesson on how to steam a pair of pants? Even I wanted a distraction from that.

Uneasy friction danced in my chest, like tiny bolts of lightning pricking. But I couldn't complain. Not even to Sammie.

It was only the first day.

I stretched out on the spotted pony ottoman and sent her a GIF of a grinning sheep holding two thumbs up. My head hung off the edge, giving me an upside-down view of the Wall. This way, the drawings were a bunch of wide pants legs, skinny pants legs, and a touch of color where a skirt or shorts stopped showing brown legs without shoes—I never drew shoes, too much detail. To see the whole outfit, I either had to roll my eyes back farther or . . .

I flipped back onto my stomach, watched as they all returned to normal.

It was that simple, to make it right again.

I took a breath and hit video to call Justice, hoping to turn things right side up.

As soon as the side of his face popped up on the call, Ms. Sadie yelled out, "Mari Henny, come on down here for dinner."

It was an order, not an invite.

"I'm coming," I shouted. "My bad. I'm yelling all in your face."

He laughed. "You good. What's up?"

"Nothing." He squinted at the phone like, You called to say nothing was up. I chuckled, made my voice chill, like when we ragged on people from Flo-A. "Am I tripping or was today all the way wild? I wasn't ready for the Flexx history lesson, for real."

He snorted. "No lies told."

"Marigold."

Ms. Sadie's voice prompted the words to rush out of my mouth. "I can't talk long. Ms. Sadie calling me for dinner."

His eyes brightened with interest. "What she cook tonight?"

Ms. Sadie's food for the win.

"Boy, I don't know." I moved around my room, stomping louder than necessary so Ms. Sadie would think I was on my way.

"I hope it ain't no quiz tomorrow," he said.

I sucked my teeth. "Hmmph. If it is, you got me to thank if you pass."

"True. True. You definitely put us up on game. Much respect."

My heart leapt happily. "You welcome."

He glanced over his shoulder. "The Closet is mad dope, though. I can't believe you ain't ever talk about it. That's some other level stuff."

"Where I'm dropping that in a conversation, though," I said, stroking my chin in fake thought.

He laughed, arms twitching as he manipulated the game controller. Distant sounds of mayhem floated out of his screen.

I eased my way closer to why I'd called. "Chandra requested to follow me on the Buzz."

He nodded. "Why ain't you accept it?"

I stopped mid-stomp. "How do you know I didn't accept?"

"'Cause Chandra put 'Mari didn't accept my Buzz request' and a upside-down smiley face in the chat."

Oh, so here we go. They were talking about me behind my back.

I talked over him cursing at his game monitor.

"Dang, y'all coming for me in the chat?"

He looked at the screen, annoyed. "I asked if you wanted me to add you."

"And you seemed glad when I said no," I pushed back.

His eyes rolled. "Nobody coming for you." I waited for him to say I was wrong about him being glad, but he defended Chandra instead. "But you are being a lil' bit shady. Just accept her request."

"Shady? How?" I pushed on before he could answer. "It's nothing against her. I don't be following everybody I meet."

"Man, whatever. I already trust her and Kara more than I trust some people at Flo-A."

I rolled my eyes at that. "You really need to get over that, Jus."

"And you really need to recognize how phony people at school are."

"Okay, so, everybody in Style High cool just because they're not rich or whatever?" I scowled at his profile.

He argued without glancing my way.

"I didn't say that. But at least everybody's real."

I pressed. "Real how?"

"Nobody fronting. We all there for the same reason."

"You mean, how we are at school?" I raised my eyebrow at the back of his neck.

I didn't hear him sigh, but his shoulders seemed to rise then fall before he said—in a voice like he was explaining to a five-year-old—"It's not the same. But go off, I guess."

I wanted to ask him why he was defending two people he'd only known for a whole day. And how come nothing I said was right, all of a sudden?

I went to my door, opened it, and yelled down, "I'm just cleaning up, real quick."

I ignored Ms. Sadie's retort—"That's a first"—and confessed, "I mean, Chandra seems cool. I'm just not ready to have her up in my Buzz timeline. You gotta admit she a little pressed."

I had meant it as a joke. Well, sort of. She was nice, but it felt desperate. I was glad I hadn't said that because he came back mad serious, shrugging as he said, "I mean we all are, Mari. For us, this a big deal."

"Yeah, everybody keeps reminding me," I said sourly.

He peered at the camera. "Everybody who? Somebody come at you about it?"

The sudden edge of protectiveness in his voice made me want to cry. It was the same way he had my back that time Royal asked how many people my father had shot in the "hood." Justice had stepped right in and rattled off the number of crimes and shootings committed by

White people against Black people. Royal got a dumb look on his face and mumbled, "Geez, the prosecution rests, counselor. I was only joking."

If Justice hadn't been there, I would have ended up actually answering Royal with a disgusted "None." I wasn't good at shutting down those kind of stupid-racist-only-joking-once-you-realize-it-offended-me statements.

We were cool again. I didn't know how long it would last. And even though I didn't know what to say anymore, I shut my door quietly, leaning against it, and lowered my voice. "No, nobody came at me. It's just, my mother didn't really want me to do Style High."

His eyebrow flicked up in question. I rushed to beat the clock before Ms. Sadie made her way up the stairs. Wouldn't nothing nice happen if she had to come get me for dinner. "She said y'all might not feel like you could be yourselves around me."

I hesitated. Too much was stewing in my mind.

I couldn't trip off Chandra's high-pitch friendliness. It made my head hurt, a little. But, hey, fake it till you make it.

Kara's salty dismissal was a front. If I let her see it bothered me, she would feed off it, sort of like how the Legs did when they knew somebody was pressed to be down with them. I knew how to play that game.

It was Justice riding the fence, like he wasn't sure how to act around me, that was killing me.

I wasn't about to say that. I picked what I hoped was the safe thing to admit.

"Maybe Chandra just requested me because she think she has to or something."

The loud chatter of gun pops stopped as he paused the game and placed the phone so he was facing it.

"I'mma keep it a stack. I'm not gonna speak for her. All I know is, they both into fashion and styling. They don't care whether I'm good at basketball. They not asking me stupid questions like, Do I get chased home by drug dealers." His eyes rolled. "Style High the first time I put myself out there like this and it's around people who from where I'm from. To me, everybody feel genuine." His eyes darted left to right, like he was trying to see into the space that separated us. "I guess maybe you feel a little left out. But that's how I be feeling at Flo-A all the time, for real."

The feeling of not fitting in anywhere curled around me, cutting off my breath.

"Marigold Henrietta."

My father's voice bassed, too close for comfort.

I opened my door and peeked my head out. He was at the top of the stairs, closer than I expected.

I whisper pleaded, "Daddy, I'm on a call. I'll be down in a minute, I promise."

His mouth crimped, like he was stuck between trying to be strict and laughing. "Me and Justice talking about how today went," I added.

He smiled, big. "Hurry up. Me and your mother would like to know how you thought it went too."

He retreated down the stairs, grumbling, "I had to threaten to whip her, Ms. Sadie."

Ms. Sadie never took anything as a joke. "Ain't no sense in whipping her now, since you ain't bother when she was young enough for it to take."

I turned my attention just in time to catch Justice saying, "I don't know nothing about if anybody think they can't be themselves around you . . ."

"Would you tell me if they did, for real?" I searched his face. Something flickered, then was gone when he said, "Mari, nobody trying hide nothing from you. If you want me add you to the group chat I will. If you don't, then don't keep putting me in the middle pressing me to tell you what somebody saying or not."

He pierced me with a steady stare until I turned away, pretending to take care of an itch on my neck. When I looked back, he was deep in finishing his thought.

"I'm just saying, you gotta relax. I don't think nobody care about your cred. . . ." He laughed. "All right, Chandra care a lil' bit. But I feel like if anybody was gonna trip over something, it would be if you wasn't doing the same thing we all doing. It ain't like Marques gave you special treatment."

"Big facts," I said, eager to agree with something, anything, at this point.

"And you already know, I'm straight stanning your pops and moms, right now."

"One hundred percent," I said, glad when he laughed.

"I got mad appreciation for this. Let them know."

"Okay, wait." I frowned. "You wouldn't want me snitching if you or somebody else didn't like something about the program, right?"

"Affirmative," he said. The faint sounds of war started. He was only half listening again. It didn't stop me. He'd said his piece and now I needed to say mine.

"Exactly. I'm not gonna play messenger girl, telling them what y'all like or don't like." I couldn't help adding, "So make sure you let everybody know."

"Nope. 'Cause I'm not playing messenger boy either." He glanced into the camera. "So, for real, last time I'm gon' ask. Do you want be in the chat or not?"

Yes.

I wanted to be part of the group. Really part of it, not tacked onto the end, the annoying extra who was only there 'cause my parents owned the company.

Except, that's who I was.

CHAPTER .10.

Marques stayed true to his threat and kicked off the next morning with the single most boring part of the job—introducing us to the librarian, Ms. Tonya, whose real title was Inventory Coordinator. Yawn.

I'm positive that the library orientation was meant to make us crave being anywhere but there, even locked in the storeroom.

Why it took three hours? I couldn't say. The entire orientation amounted to: the Closet was the pretty side of Flexx. A big store where you could see yourself shopping. But somebody had to gather all those things and get them ready for display. And that somebody was us.

He shipped us off to the storeroom, trusting us to divide the tasks "democratically."

Clearly, Marques had never witnessed a bunch of teenagers in a group project trying to decide who was going to do what. Democracy isn't the word I'd use for the process.

I figured we'd hit "Not It" until we ran out of jobs we couldn't take.

We walked in a tight cluster down the hallway leading to the storeroom, like we were going into a haunted house. I stopped dead in my tracks when we opened the door. Chandra smashed into me. Kara had enough sense to ease around us. Justice whistled, a high-pitched wowwww.

Somehow a tornado had blown through and left the rest of the building untouched.

Clothes were everywhere. Some hanging up neatly and others that seemed purposely thrown any- and everywhere in and around bins, hanging every which way off racks.

Our work area was obvious—a long metal table, surrounded by chairs, in between four big metal columns that ran to the sky-high ceiling. The table had shoes all over it and a couple million pins, paper clips, and plastic inventory tags. A clipboard hung from one of the columns. Next to it sat a fat blue bubble with a long black hose. The hose had a weird white head at the end. The steamer. It looked like a vacuum and an alien had a baby.

"Who left it like this?" Justice asked. His hand ran down the back of his head, petting himself like it would conjure the answer. He turned from one mess to another, taking it all in.

"The interns, probably," I guessed. "I never really come back here."

"Of course you don't," Kara said, low-loud like when you want somebody to hear you.

I pushed past the dryness in my mouth, falling for her trap.

"What does that mean?" I asked.

Kara opened her mouth to answer but Justice over-talked her.

"It's like they made a mess on purpose," he said, kicking a pair of shorts by his feet.

"So, it's like . . . we're being hazed?" Chandra asked. She looked over her shoulder like a hidden camera crew was going to jump out and yell, "Sike!" "Do we have to clean this up?"

I sighed. "I guess that's what putting stuff back in inventory means."

"You guess?" Kara said, eyes rolling

"She's never worked here," Chandra said, jumping to my defense. "Right, Mari?"

I nodded at Chandra, pushing away the urge to run up to my parents' suite of offices and quit.

We all congregated around the table. The smell of defeat on us mixed with the ever-present stink of plastic that haunted the storeroom.

Rows and rows and rows of clothes racked to the ceiling went deeper than the eye could see. Ladders, long-reaching poles, and three-stair stepping stools were all over the place. There were cubbies for shoes. A large white wall with holes and pegs for belts, jewelry, hats, and other headgear. It was a never-ending sea of clothes.

Since this was everybody's dream job, I didn't think anybody was going to say how they felt. Day two of assignments nobody signed up for. But Kara wasn't having it.

"The part of the job that sucks, for real, has just entered the chat." She scooted a metal chair out from the table. I winced at the scraping sound it made against the concrete floor.

Chandra chimed in. "I get that we need to learn the ropes a little. . . ." She gazed around the room sullenly, taking it all in. Her arms seemed to wrap around her tiny body twice as she hugged herself. "But how they gonna stick us in a dungeon the rest of the day?"

We were surrounded by enough clothes to furnish a small mall. But Marques and Joel had made it clear: we wouldn't be doing anything for a while but keeping the Closet stocked and the storeroom well-organized. And we had a binder full of instructions on how, to prove it.

I wasn't sure what was worst, being here in the bowels of the building or out in the Closet watching more senior style associates do what we thought we'd be.doing.

I wanted to put the trainees on blast for expecting to walk in and take over. I also wanted to agree with them. I mean, I was stuck too.

Things were ready to turn into a full-blown pity party when Justice laid it out.

"I'm not saying I love that we basically the clean-up crew, but . . ." He picked up a pointy white inventory tag and tapped at the table. "Try dropping out. I bet they'd call the next best person on the list with the quickness."

"I'm not saying I'm doing all that," Chandra said, sulkiness gone. "Just . . . I didn't think we'd be on janitor's duty. I did enough of that last summer, when—"

"How 'bout we get started before Marques or Joel come check on us," Justice interrupted. He grabbed the assignment sheet off the table, taking charge. "Come on,

Kara, I'll be on steam duty. You do shoe and accessories till I have enough stuff for you to check back into inventory. Mari, you and Chandra can get stuff from upstairs and bring it back."

I clicked my heels and saluted. "Well, yes sir."

"You good with that?" he asked, frowning.

"I'm fine with it, Mr. Supervisor," I said. A tantrum sat in my chest, ready to explode. I headed to the door, calling behind me, "Ready, Chandra?"

Her footsteps skittered behind me as she caught up.

Before the door closed, I heard Kara say, "Umph, she big mad."

CHAPTER .11.

The farther we got from the storeroom the worse I felt.

Justice hadn't even thought to pair us up.

Or he could have picked what he wanted to do, then asked me what I wanted. Ride or die get first pick, the rando chicks get what's left. But no, he just threw me with Chandra like . . .

Like he didn't want to be paired with me. It stung.

I clenched my teeth against the feeling of betrayal and forced myself to silently chant:

He was at Flexx to work. We were at Flexx to work.

Getting mad was a bad look.

I had to get it together.

The style floor looked like any other ordinary

office—a long stretch of hall that squared around a nation of cubes with desks. The walls were too tall to see over. People, on their way to more glamorous tasks than ours, squeezed by us and the wheeled cart we pushed. Every now and then, someone would pop out of their door-less office. If they recognized me, they smiled, greeted me by name. But there were plenty I didn't know. I hadn't hung out at Flexx regularly much since sixth grade. Those who didn't know me knew we weren't important enough to waste time on and went about their business like we weren't there blocking the hall with our bulky cart.

Chandra and I walked down a long row of cubicles. White plastic bins were lined in front of them like short garbage cans. I was in charge of dumping whatever was in the bins into the cart. She was the chief cart pusher and made sure that if the person in the cubicle had checked out clunky heels, clunky heels were what we picked up. Long strings of words streamed out of her mouth until we reached a new bin, then she'd quietly check the list against the clothing to make sure it was right. Guess I was silent one minute too long.

"Are you good?" she asked.

"Yeah," I said cheerfully.

Nothing to see here. Justice not curbing me or nothing. So, so good over here.

"Were you and Justice a couple or something?" She laughed, then covered her mouth, muffling her giggles. "Sorry. I didn't mean to come out so nosy like that. It just seem like . . . I don't know." She paused. "It's like, you still friends and all. But maybe there's a juicy story behind why you not together no more." She cheesed at me. "Dish."

I was close to admitting exactly how it felt having my closest friend act like I was some rando chick he happened to also go to school with. It was too humiliating. And I didn't know her from a hole in the wall.

I swear, I spent too much time with Ms. Sadie. I even thought in Ms. Sadie soundbites.

"No tea to spill," I said, hoping it had the right amount of nonchalance in it. "We're just friends."

"Oh, my bad." Chandra glanced over like she wasn't sure, her long neck reminding me of a giraffe. "My radar must be off. I usually read people pretty good."

Her radar was probably beeping and booping all over the place.

"Sometimes we got that brother-sister vibe, for sure." I leaned on the cart, feigning indifference. "I think Kara more his type."

My heart pounded, waiting and wanting Chandra to disagree. Guilt slithered its way into my conscience. This wasn't a competition for Justice's attention. Except, low-key, everything was a competition.

She squinted, checking in on her radar, maybe, before giving her verdict. "I mean, yesterday when we all first met he checked her out for sure. Dudes, right?" I laughed along, earning all kind of acting stripes. "But I didn't get nothing jumping off him like he was pressed."

I should have been ashamed for how happy that made me. I wasn't.

I picked up a bin full of shoes and dumped them into the cart. Chandra looked at the list on the tablet, into the cart, back at the tablet, into the cart, and back at the tablet.

It was going to take all day if she checked everything five times.

I raised my eyebrow. "Everything right?"

Her laugh was a high bird chirp. "Oh yeah. Just making sure."

"Cool," I said, already on to the next bin. I'd picked it up, ready to dump it when she said, "Hold on."

Her eyes scanned the tablet. She sorted through some items in the cart and nodded.

"Umm . . . now?" I asked, trying to be funny.

She nodded, face serious.

I emptied the bin and moved to the next one.

It took me a second to realize Chandra wasn't following me. I walked back to her.

"My bad. Is everything there?" I asked.

Silence while she counted.

She checked, checked again, then started pushing the cart.

She didn't look at me as she said, "I don't want to get yelled at if things are missing. Know what I mean?"

My cheeks burned.

"No. You're right. I was on autopilot."

I picked up the next bin, held it for her so she could do the checking. I was fine as her eyes went from the bin to the tablet the first two times, but by the third time I was over it.

As soon as she gave me the go-ahead, I dumped the bin, clanging it against the cart hard, and walked ahead.

She cleared her throat. "Am I taking too long to check the list?"

"Huh? Oh, no," I lied.

She caught up to me. "I'm probably being a little obsessive. But you have no idea. Like, this job is—" I followed her gaze down the hall. There were bins outside of every cubicle. We were going to be here all day. Finally she met my curious eyes. "It's a thousand times better than what I did last year. I'm trying not to screw it up."

"How about I push the cart," I said when we got to the next cubicle.

She picked up the bin, accepting my offer.

I waited, patiently this time, then pushed on when she dumped. We took our time then, strolling past a string of empty bins. Without inventory to worry about for a few minutes, her words streamed nonstop.

"My mom is the director of facilities at Bradley. She's in charge of the janitors and landscapers. So, she got me a job helping to clean last year." Her laugh was light, like scrubbing somebody's toilet was no big deal. "It was between that and gardening. But I have mad allergies so mopping floors was the winner."

I didn't know how she could laugh about mopping floors.

"When I got the Style High acceptance letter you would have thought I'd won a million dollars the way I acted a fool." She grinned ear to ear. "I thought we were going to jump right into styling or at least play with hooking up outfits. I'm disappointed that we haven't, but even this is better than cleaning up classrooms."

There were two full bins in a row. She fell into deep concentration.

I peeked into the nearby cubicles. A lot were deserted. Most people were in client meetings or downstairs in the Closet working. A few were at their computers or on the phone. Music streamed from different directions. Somebody was playing Killer Joe, somebody else jazz, and somebody had the sounds of waves crashing. I guess everybody was used to everybody's else's music and barely heard it.

"All right, so you and Justice not a couple. But do you want y'all to be?" Chandra asked, poking me into the present with her question.

"Well, it's only one other Black dude in our grade. I can't be that picky," I said.

"I know that's right," Chandra said, waving her hand like she was testifying in church. "It's three dudes at Bradley, all on the basketball team. I be so tired of people trying to hook me up with one of them. Like, I'm good over here."

Before Justice came, people at Flo-A stayed trying to pair me and Milton up. I was as horrified by the idea as he was. It had to be mad tiring trying to be White all day. I didn't want no parts of that. I couldn't even imagine what Ms. Sadie would think if I called myself bringing him home. Did Milton even eat soul food? The idea made me smile. Chandra mistook it for my answer. "Oh, see, my radar never wrong. I knew something was between y'all."

My head shook vigorously. "Huh. No. For real, friends is friends is friends and that's all we are."

The last thing I needed was her running and telling Justice—or worst, Justice and Kara— that I was crushing on him.

Chandra balanced a bin on the edge of the cart. Her brown eyes, big and wondering, were intent.

"Did you help him get into Style High?" She rushed ahead. "I'm being nosy again. My bad."

"I didn't even know he had applied until last week," I said, ignoring the hard pit in my stomach.

"Hmmph, he good, then," she said. "I'm not gonna lie. If me and you went to school together, I can't promise I wouldn'ta asked for that hookup."

She grinned. To show she was joking or to soften the blow that she wouldn't have had no problem using me, I couldn't tell. Points for honesty, but dang.

I nodded at the bin. "You should probably check that so we can move on. We still have the whole other side of cubicle nation to do."

"Ha ha. Cubicle nation. But, true." She did her eleventy hundred double checks. "I definitely can't be caught slacking while I'm working with you."

"You heard Marques, I'm no different than anybody else this summer," I said.

"But you are." She waved my words away. "Even if he treats you like he treats us, it's because your parents gave him permission to. You know? Shoot, the dean's daughter, at Bradley, is the same year as me. We had a few classes together, this year. I see how the teachers treat her. Like they treat the rest of us . . . but not."

"It's like that with legacies at Flowered," I admitted. "But not here. Flexx has its own rules. Trust."

"I didn't mean any harm by saying that, Marigold." She looked genuinely worried that I was mad. She put her hand on my shoulder. "You not nothing like Lorel, Dean Jarrett's daughter. She definitely plays the game, letting people think she's cool but then the teachers say stuff sometimes and I know it has to come from her yapping."

It was funny since yapping was the perfect way to describe Chandra's nonstop chatter. She took my smile to mean it was all good.

"I'm just saying, we all know you're the same but different." She placed the empty bin on the floor, positioning it perfectly in its own nook like even having it crooked would be a mark against her. We walked side by side down the next hall, which was plump with full white bins.

The cart was swollen with items. A silver stiletto, separated from its partner, bobbed on top of a tangle of skirts. We'd have to head back to the storeroom soon to unload. I started to suggest that maybe we do that now, but Chandra picked up a bin and said, "When you gonna join the group chat?" She shook her head. "My bad. Never mind. Justice said you probably wouldn't." She stopped talking while she did her work. Her words picked up like they'd never paused once she emptied the bin into the cart. "Just know I'm totally wit' it for you to join. I'm me no matter who's around." She cocked her head in thought, then laughed. "And keeping it one hundred, Kara probably is too. So, just saying, you should go on and slide into our DMs."

She was off to the next cubicle, laughing at her own joke, too deep in her zone to catch my silent wonder.

CHAT-TER

Mari_Golden:

You told everybody what I said to you
about my mother thinking y'all can't be
yourself around me? 😠

JayRocks:

👀 What's wrong w/that?

Mari_Golden:

Umm, cause it's nobody's business?
Cause I only told you since you keep
asking bout me joining the chat and I
was trying keep it a stack why I won't.

JayRocks:

There u go. You really tripping over
the chat thing. I wish I hadn't told
you about it.

Mari_Golden:

I wish you hadn't either. And nobody
tripping. But I tell u why I'm not joining
and u run and tell them? Y'all don't got
nothing else better to talk about than
me?

JayRocks:

You on one, for real.

Mari_Golden:

people probably already think I'm
telling everything I see

JayRocks:

Nobody think that.

Mari_Golden:

Kara probably do. 😒

JayRocks:

lol it took 2 whole days for u to
come for her

Mari_Golden:

Me come for her?! She walked in
swinging.

JayRocks:

She didn't tho. You just want
everybody to like you.

Mari_Golden:

I don't care if she like me

JayRocks:

You do tho. It's why you let them
plastics at school say whatever
out their mouth w/o checking 'em.

You put up w/dat mess every day.
But Kara ain't falling over to be
your friend & you ready peace out
on her after two days. It's wack.
She good peoples.

Mari_Golden:
. . . alright Jus.

JayRocks:
I'm serious, Mari.

Mari_Golden:
Yup. I figured.

JayRocks:
Look, Chandra kept asking why u
wasn't in the chat. I told the truth.
My bad. 😬

Mari_Golden:
👍

CHAPTER .12.

I think some people slept at Flexx. There was always activity, no matter how early you arrived or late you stayed.

When I walked in the next morning, the Closet was already jumping. Instead of music, the drone of voices and squeaking wheels of clothes racks being moved around were their own melody. I peeped at the racks me and Chandra had set up based on requests from the style associates. I admired our handiwork, watching as the associates went over every item, checking it against their requests.

Check if you want, I thought. There won't be any mistakes. Chandra made sure of that.

While we were racking the clothes, I'd felt like shaking

her for being so nitpicky. But in the end, I was confident we hadn't missed a single item or pulled an azure-colored blouse when the request was for turquoise.

I couldn't take the credit for the thoroughness, but felt an odd sense of pride, anyway. The good feeling didn't last long. The closer I got to our hub, the tighter my throat got.

I had almost told Mommy I didn't feel like coming in today. The only thing that would have gotten me out of it would have been cramps. Periods were never around when you needed them.

So, here I was.

I decided Justice had one more chance to curb me before I . . .

I didn't think out exactly what I would do. Hoped I wouldn't need to.

I picked my head up, working to walk with confidence, letting the energy of the room push my feet faster than I felt like walking.

I passed by Ms. Tonya meeting with her staff at a station of computers, their screens grids of columns and rows, filled with inventory information. I shuddered, hoping one of our tasks wouldn't be entering data into the computer.

By the time I arrived at our hub, Chandra was already

at her desk. Her mass of braids, in a huge, fluffy side pony, wiggled as she waved at me.

Justice had his arm around one of our mannies, taking pics of himself. He nodded my way. It wasn't much. But he hadn't ignored me. My heart was stupid happy about it.

I scoured the area for Kara and was relieved she wasn't there yet. Justice could defend her all he wanted, she changed the whole vibe. Girls like her always did.

"Morning," Chandra chirped.

Her cheerfulness was a shot of caffeine to my mood. "Hey." No chirping back, but I was friendlier—pushing the energy into the air, hoping it swirled around Justice and reminded him that in four weeks after these two girls were a memory, it would still be me and him.

I tucked my bag under my desk. Seeing Justice ready to take another pic, I ran across the room, clearing the space in enough time to thrust myself into the shot.

"You got a little speed on you for being a Hill chick," Justice teased.

I wrinkled my nose at him. Then let it go. He'd never called me a Hill chick before.

"You already know," I said, flexing. "First place at last year's Regionals."

"What events you run?" Chandra asked, forever

curious. Not like my favorite color, ice cream, and things I did besides be Manita and Marshall Johnson's daughter hadn't been covered in interviews before. Something told me Chandra had probably had done a good ol' Google by now. I played along anyway.

"The 100 and the 400 relay," I said. I stepped away enough so Justice could get back to snapping solo pics.

"You do hurdles?" Chandra asked.

I made a face.

"It's an acquired skill," Justice said, without boasting.

"Me and my skinned knees know it, too," I said. Just the memory of tripping over the hurdles, that one and only time, made my legs hurt. "You run track?"

"Never that," Chandra said. "Slide me a book or sketch pad and I'm good."

My head whipped to Justice. Sketch pad. Had he told her about my Wall? Like stop giving this girl ways to jock me.

He looked over my head in the direction of the elevator then made a low woo-whoop sound as he took his seat.

I froze, confused for a second, before I realized that was the signal that Joel and Marques were making their way to us.

When I turned, Kara was at her desk, arms folded in front of her.

When had she arrived?

I started to say, "Hey," as I walked by, but she was looking past me.

"What up, Kara?" Justice said as he eased into his seat, beside hers.

"Hey," she said.

I listened for an extra hint of friendliness. But it was just a hey. Maybe the same one she would have given me if I'd spoken. She didn't send off friendly vibes, but maybe I wasn't either.

Her hair was pulled back into a tight ballerina bun, right above her neck. A long pair of jeweled chandelier earrings swept across her shoulders. She was wearing a white tee shirt with the face of a panda in black jewels. A piece from the Flexx spring collection.

The outfit was way more subdued than the one she'd worn the day before. But the Holly Heights touch was in the pink, glittery lip gloss. It was so thick, it made me squint. Fashion restraint just wasn't in her vocabulary.

She must have said something to Justice, because he smiled, then shook his head. I leaned in, not really aware I was doing it, trying to catch their conversation. Of course, that's when she turned her head my way.

We sat there for a few seconds, staring at each other.

Her unflinching, me blinking fast. This time I spoke and even managed a smile that probably looked as tight and forced as it felt.

"'Sup," she said, turning her head away.

My breath hissed out slowly.

It wasn't the worst start but wasn't exactly my idea of starting over fresh either.

Clap, clap, clap.

Marques stepped into our hub.

He really thought he was some kind of teacher.

"Good morning, young ones," he said, prim.

Joel was the cheerful opposite. "Morn-inng."

Everyone's attention sharpened as Joel wheeled over a cart overflowing with random, mostly ugly clothes. There were overly designed tops. Belts that had no good reason to be made because they wouldn't complement anything. Simple tops and bottoms that if we paired them up would probably get us thrown out of the program—since anyone could combine a T-shirt and shorts.

Joel's hands flew to his hips.

"Good stylists need clothes that already look nice. But great stylists can make anything work. Even this stuff." He wrinkled his nose at the pile of clothes like they were wriggling maggots. "I don't expect greatness, yet." He paused for effect. "But let's see how well you do under pressure."

He strolled around as he talked, stopping behind me.

"Two people will come up and do their best to make these rags into haute couture." The last two words—hoat coo tour—flew at us on his breath. He stopped behind Justice's chair. "Actually, if you can make these into high fashion I'm out of a job." He laughed. Marques didn't crack a smile. Joel cleared his throat, his jowly cheeks frozen in a happy face. "We're looking to see who can make the best of the least. Simple, right?"

A collective head bob from the group.

"We're not here for simple," Marques said. He flipped open the cover of his tablet and nestled it in the crook of his arm. He swiped at the screen and held it up like a librarian at story hour so we could see the glow of a stopwatch. "You'll have five minutes."

Life was super competitive at Flo-A. No way these challenges could be any worse, until Joel said, "Marigold and Justice, take your places at the cart."

It flew out of my mouth before I could stop it. "Can't I go against Chandra?"

Her face fell.

Kara snorted. "Ohhh, she saying you the weakest link, Chandra."

I yelled down the line at her. "No, I'm not." I put my hand on Chandra's desk, patting it to console her. "That's not what I meant. It's that—" I begged Joel, making up my excuse as it threaded itself together in my head. "Me and Justice already know each other from school. I should go up against somebody who don't already know my game."

"Scared I'mma whup up on you?" Justice said, supremely confident, of course.

"I don't care who I go up against," Chandra said, arms crossed.

"That's right, don't let her carry you like that," Kara said, enjoying the chaos.

"It doesn't matter to me if the three of y'all are friends, become friends, or whatever." Marques sucked in air and then blew it out his nose, quick. "If you ever want to do more than fill style orders or clean up the storeroom, we need to see what you got. Let's go."

I stepped up, already spying a few items I wanted. Justice put one hand on the mani, readying himself.

I did the same.

"Cheering one another on is allowed," Joel said.

"Go!" Marques barked, with no one, two, three, ready, set, or anything.

I grabbed an oversized sheer navy-blue scarf. I pinched it in my fingers, holding tight. My eyes roamed the cart, searching for something to build around my find.

In the distance, I heard Chandra shouting my name over and over, like I was a horse racing down a track. It sounded like she was bouncing in her chair. I was grateful for the support. Surprisingly, Kara stayed neutral, choosing a generic "Come on, y'all. Do it. Come on."

Justice buzzed around me. He picked a piece, draped it on the manny. Picked a piece, draped it. I was vaguely aware that his manny was at least draped while mine stood nude. I stayed in the rabbit hole until the shouts around me were hollow. I zoned in on the pieces of clothing, now jostled and hanging out of the cart from Justice's frantic snatching. An American flag disguised as a tank top swam to the top of the pile. I grabbed it.

"Oooh, okay, not sure where she going with that," Chandra said with a nervous giggle.

I shook her voice out of my head and dug through the cart, making a pile on top of the clothes Justice was searching.

"Nice. Make it harder for him to find stuff," Kara said, momentarily forgetting she hated me.

Finally, at the bottom of the pile, I found what I was looking for—a pair of off-white short-shorts. It wasn't perfect, but close enough. I grabbed them and tended to the manny.

"Three minutes," Marques said calmly.

"Three minutes," Joel repeated.

"Come on, Mari. Justice is almost done," Chandra yelled.

I wriggled the shorts up the mani, then panicked. No way they'd stay up by themselves.

I let them fall down and headed back to the bin for a clip.

I bunched the shorts from the back and snapped the clip in place.

I pulled the tank top over the mannequin's headless form—dithering with it until it fell just right.

"Two minutes," Marques said.

I exhaled to shake the nerves.

I crisscrossed the scarf into a makeshift sarong. My hands trembled as I worked to get it in place. The fabric slipped, refusing to cooperate. With a minute left, I raced to the cart, this time digging in with both hands until I found a belt. Didn't matter what it looked like.

I ran back to my manny with Marques quietly counting

down, Kara and Chandra helping him along, chanting, "Ten, nine, eight . . ."

I cinched the gold chain-link belt, which some other decade had rejected, around the manny's waist until it held the sarong in place, right before Marques snapped, "Time's up!"

I stood back looking at our work, heart racing, knees wobbling.

Justice put his fist out and I dapped it up with a bump.

"That was crazy," he said, breathing as hard as me.

"Back to your seats, little birds," Joel directed.

A chorus of "good jobs" rang out as we sat down.

Marques and Joel walked around our mannequins, looking them up and down.

My stomach shriveled in on itself. Suddenly it wasn't about winning. I was just afraid of the feedback. Justice's face told me he felt the same. We shared a look of quiet panic, then waited.

Marques and Joel exchanged a few whispered words.

"Who won?" Kara asked.

"There's no winning right now," Marques said in a disappointed voice. I don't know if he was upset that he couldn't pick a winner or that Kara didn't know better.

"Only critiques," he continued. "We'll start with you, Chandra. Your thoughts?"

Chandra's eyes widened. Then she composed herself, looked at each mannequin, and stammered a critique. Thumbs-up for the scarf that came down just below the shorts, like a sheer dress.

Marques sucked his teeth. "We're going to play softball and only say what we like?" He hugged his tablet to his chest. His gaze was stern. "Look, if a client hates your work they're going to say so. They don't care if you love it. Or if it's the hottest trend right now. If they hate it, they'll hate it. You're in the program, so I assume you can put an outfit together."

His eyes studied us, appraising our clothes.

I found myself doing the same, trying to see what he saw.

Everybody was already dressed Flexx appropriate. Business attire at Flexx was about how well an outfit was put together—preferably built around at least one piece from a Jus' Flexx collection.

Our crew had fallen in line.

Justice wore Bermuda shorts—from this year's collection—with a crisp, ironed, not-a-single-wrinkle T-shirt. His tennas were toothbrush clean. Chandra wore a Jus' Flexx sundress, with roses blooming all over it, that showed her tiny shoulders. It was one of the line's most popular last year. In the dark, the roses glowed.

Finding nothing bad to say, Marques went on in his exhausted professor way.

"Look, you dressed yourselves. You look fine. But that doesn't have anything to do with styling someone else."

He stopped talking and Joel stepped in on cue.

"Marigold, your outfit is on point." His hand came up the second I allowed myself to grin. "But makeshift sarongs are a nuisance. Clients never know how to keep them wrapped neatly. They fall off the shoulders. They come unwrapped. You sit down and the wrap goes off-kilter." He frowned in frustration like my wrap was doing all those things as he spoke. "I like that it has an easy look to it. But it's a hard look to maintain."

I felt the crew's eyes on me.

Chandra reached over and patted my desk, the same way I'd consoled her earlier.

The lump in my throat began to swell and I willed myself to stay eyes straight. If I turned and saw anyone pitying me, or worse, smirking, I'd burst into tears.

Thankfully, Joel moved on to Justice, picking his outfit apart just as cleanly.

Chandra and Kara didn't have it any easier when their turn came.

We went like that all day. Paired and timed. Timed and paired, until our critiques were brutally honest and M and J were satisfied that our skin was thicker than when we'd started.

CHAPTER .13.

I took the elevator from the bowels of the building to the top floor. My parents' office suite gave new meaning to the words "there's levels to this." The doors opened to a bright private lobby and a half-moon reception desk. The words Flexx Unlimited were in big block silver letters on the wall behind it. Silence filled the lobby. It was an area that people only came to when invited. Luwanda, the receptionist, had the world's easiest job. All she did was direct people or calls to Janine and Antwan, my dad's and mom's assistants.

I don't know how she didn't lose her mind in the quiet.

I whispered automatically, not wanting to break up the silence. "Hey, Ms. Lu."

She was in her thirties, probably the same age as my

parents. If you went by what you could see from in front of the desk, you'd think she was skinny. She had a sharp chin, a thin neck, and a head full of locs that she had half up and half down. She also had unusually large hips that made it look like somebody had fused two different bodies together.

She came around the desk to give me a hug. Her locs tickled my face.

"Hey, Marigold. I haven't seen you in a few months."

"Yeah, school keeps me busy," I said, the answer practiced by now.

I had lived at Flexx after school when I was in elementary. Mostly staying either in the Closet or lounging on one of the sofas in my mom's or dad's office, watching shows on my phone. But Flo-A didn't play once you got in sixth grade. It was mandatory to do a sport and serve on one of the student body committees. Some people claim they're busy. I really was, between homework, track, and the I & D Committee.

That's Inclusion & Diversity and don't get me started. News flash—diversity doesn't mean the same thing to everybody.

Ms. Lu's hug was a homecoming. She smelled like blueberries and honey. She always gave my mother homemade shampoos to try, causing Ms. Sadie to fuss, "Go 'head and keep putting any ol' thing in your hair. Gon' wake up bald, one of these days."

Ms. Lu's hair hadn't fallen out yet. Still, Mommy usually only pretended to use them.

It was good to be missed. I humored her by catching her up.

Yes, Style High was "nice" so far.

Yeah, it was cool that my parents were doing this.

No, I didn't know her oldest was going to be a freshman at Poncey High.

Yes, I was excited to go into upper school next year. That got a little laugh and a "Oh excuse me, not just high school but upper school" out of her. I forget that everybody didn't necessarily speak Flowered Arms.

I guess my eye wandered past her because she politely wrapped it up.

"Not sure which of your parents you came to see, but you're in luck." She hobbled back to her station, like one leg was shorter than the other, and waved to the right. "Your mom's in there with your dad. Go on in."

Janine wasn't at her desk. Probably gone for the day. Her area just outside of Daddy's office included a desk, a file cabinet, and a single uncomfortable chair. Visitors were expected and didn't linger. It was so neat and serene, her desk free of papers or clutter, it was hard to tell anybody worked there. The Manita Johnson effect, for sure. Mommy had a real thing for cluttered desks and I had a secret pile of papers stowed away in my closet to prove it. Most days it was easier to stuff things there than actually try and keep my desk organized.

The double doors to my dad's office were diagonal to Janine's desk. No one was getting by her unless she said so. One of the doors was cracked open. As I started to enter, my mother's voice carried through the opening.

I hesitated at the tightness in her tone and the way she clipped her words like her tongue was slicing them.

"Fine, Marshall. Your mind is made up. And, as usual, you—"

"Why it gotta be 'as usual,' Manita? You acting like I'm being unreasonable."

Anytime he called Mommy by her real name, it wasn't nothing good. We could be home talking about a TV show and somehow it would turn to something about Flexx and next thing you know they were Manita and Marshalling each other trying to get their point across.

That Metro ride was starting to sound better, but I was trapped.

I wasn't in the mood to play referee, if I stayed. Ms. Lu would wonder why I was done so quick, if I left.

The door shuddered, cracking open another inch. I put on a smile to pretend I'd just gotten there but then nobody came out. My mother spoke again, businesslike, but there was something else in her voice too.

Worry?

"You are being unreasonable. I didn't want to do this, remember? You did. And then you tied my hands, making it impossible for us to ask Marigold anything."

"Come on, Nut, I didn't make it impossible. If something goes sideways you know she's gonna tell us."

I couldn't believe Mommy was still fussing about me being a part of the program. How much damage did she think I could do to these Flexx super fans? If cleaning up every day after all the stylists hadn't run them off, I doubted there was anything I could do to "ruin" it now.

And what kind of drama qualified as going sideways? 'Cause if Kara being a hater counted, I had plenty to tell them. I knew it didn't. Her hating wasn't the same as the time Hunter Mason kept telling racist jokes and when I wouldn't laugh, told me that I shouldn't get mad because I wasn't from the ghetto so he wasn't telling jokes about me. That had been fifth grade. And when I told my mother, she legit lost her stuff. Went up to the school and told the dean that if Hunter wasn't suspended for violating the school's code of conduct on respecting others, then the next contribution she and Daddy would make to the school was an independent audit of the faculty's ability to deal with racism and bigotry.

Kara hadn't called me out my name. We just weren't getting along. Yet?

My mother caught the honey in Daddy's voice. He was trying to loosen her up and she wasn't having it.

"Don't do that, Marshall. I want to make sure Mari is okay with this."

"Joel and Marques would let us know if something was up. It sounds like everybody is getting along," Daddy said.

To my face, my mother was always super practical. But I'd seen her go Momma Bear at the parent advisory meetings and with the dean if she thought they were on some nonsense that hurt "students of color," which was code for me. I mean me and a small handful of others. But mostly me. Knowing she was worried put me in my feelings.

I felt bad for thinking Mommy only cared about the other trainees.

"Who wants to give me a ride home?" I sang, making my entrance.

Mommy's eyebrows stretched to her hairline.

"Marigold. You scared me, luv."

I stood in between them, facing my mom. Daddy's big office spread out around us, a fishbowl with gorgeous city views.

"Ay, look who it is." Daddy presented his cheek to me and I kissed it. "Just in time to put your mother at ease." He placed his hands on my shoulders. "This looks like a happy style trainee to me."

I rolled my eyes. "Can you really put style in front of it if I been locked in the storeroom half the day?"

"They'll release y'all from the bowels of the building in due time," Daddy said. He gave my shoulders a light squeeze and walked over to his desk, his point proven. Mommy was another story. She gave him a look, clearly not happy that he'd moved on, then turned her attention to me.

"Are things going well? I'm not asking you to sni—" She blew a breath and corrected herself. "To tell on anyone. Are you getting along with everyone?"

Daddy looked up, his attention back on us.

I hadn't seen my mother this worried since the

seventh-grade field trip to Montreal, when Brett Curtis called me Brown Sugar Shaquita and threw dollar bills at me and told me to shake my Black butt. Worry was after she'd laid his mother out, though. Every parent-chaperone on that trip heard my mother tell Ms. Curtis that if Brett ever called me anything but my name, he would find out just how hip-hop the Johnsons could get.

That's when I realized the only thing scarier than corporate Manita was from-the-streets Manita.

To this day, Brett kept his distance. He didn't want none of Manita Johnson.

And usually neither did my father. But when he got locked in on something, he had a way of going all in. He had backed me joining Style High. I couldn't call what me and Kara were doing getting along, but I couldn't tell the truth either. Not now when worry was etched into my mother's face, her eyes looking me up and down like she was searching for bruises.

"It's good, for real." I caught my father's nod of affirmation and ventured further, trying to avoid telling an outright lie. "Everybody's . . . cool."

"Told you," my father said with a clap.

My mother's lips tightened in a silent, Shut up,

Marshall. She smiled genuinely at me. "I'm glad y'all are becoming friends."

I opened my mouth to object. I hadn't said all that. But her face had lost that worried look, so I let it be.

"Come on. Daddy has a west coast conference call. Me and you can get Tony's."

She said the last word loud in Daddy's direction, knowing she'd get a reaction at the mention of his favorite restaurant.

He fake pouted. "Y'all wrong. How you gonna go to Tony's without me?"

"We're celebrating," Mommy said.

His eyebrow rose. "What? Me being right?"

Mommy laughed. "Bye, Pea."

"Ms. Sadie gonna be hot, with y'all eating out in the middle of the week," he hollered after us.

He wasn't wrong. Ms. Sadie laid into us good when we came home with tiny silver boxes of leftovers. But it was worth it. Sometimes after a hard day's work, you gotta treat yourself. I needed all the fuel I could get to make good on the lie my mother believed . . . me becoming friends with Kara.

CHAT-TER

Mari_Golden:

Hey, I wasn't tryna say you didn't have
style skills earlier. Seriously.

> **Cha-Cha:**
> Who dis?

Mari_Golden:

My bad. It's Marigold.

> **Cha-Cha:**
> 😂😂 J/K I knew it was you. We
> tight, you alright.

Mari_Golden:

You sure? I don't want you thinking I
was throwing shade.

> **Cha-Cha:**
> 👍 I'm a Bradley girl, I've seen
> worse shade.

Mari_Golden:

ha ha same @ Flo-A. We could have a
Mean Girl Olympics.

> **Cha-Cha:**
> LOL OMG we should. Like all the
> private schools in DC.

Mari_Golden:

yes but public schools too. Not gonna lie, I think the hood schools got some gold medal contenders all day. 😆

Cha-Cha:

No lies told. I volunteer Lorel as tribute from Bradley and Kara from Banneker HS

Mari_Golden:

😄 as tribute. Yessssss! I didn't know she went to Banney. My cousin gonna be a sophomore there. They might know each other.

Cha-Cha:

Your cousin from Holly too?

Mari_Golden:

No. Marks

Cha-Cha:

Oh. Kara just gonna be a freshman. So probz not. I still say Banney getting a gold medalist. She has no problem putting people in their place. 😑

Mari_Golden:

Facts. I just wanna stay out of her way
for real. #NoDramaPlease

Cha-Cha:

You gets none from me.

Mari_Golden:

B/c this better than cleaning toilets?

Cha-Cha:

😁 ✓

Chandra being nice to me because she didn't want to mess up her summer gig should have been enough. Nice is nice, right? But it wasn't.

How I wanted our chat to go:

Mari_Golden:

#NoDramaPlease

Cha-Cha:

You gets none from me.

Mari_Golden:

B/c this better than cleaning toilets?

Cha-Cha:

True but naw, cause I rides witchu

Mari

But, for real, nobody wanted to ride with me.

CHAPTER .14.

During the morning, when we had challenges, it wasn't too bad. Marques and Joel had us competing in all kinds of wacky style games:

Blindfolding us and making us guess what material we were rubbing;

Scavenger hunts;

20 Minute Style-Out.

During the games I almost forgot nobody was riding with me. I almost forgot that after five days, Justice had said maybe three hundred words to me, directly. Probably fifty of them didn't have anything to do with getting our work done.

The afternoons were another story.

M & J shooed us to the dungeon far away from any other activity in the building. Justice had officially knighted himself some sort of supervisor—grabbing the clipboard to hand out duties like holiday packages. Every day I wanted to say something, or at least joke how he never gave anybody else a chance to be the leader. I let it ride since Kara and Chandra didn't seem bothered.

What was I going to say—When is my turn?

I sat on the high stool beside the worktable, slowly swiveling from side to side as he read off the assignments. Kara and Chandra stood on either side of him, expectant. My breathing was shallow as I waited—not quite ready to be paired with Kara.

We'd decided (well Justice had) that it only took one person to collect inventory from the Style floor. I prayed for that job. Needing the alone time.

Justice looked a foot taller than his six-foot-one frame in his extra-long dude capris. He had hooked up the white denim that belled just below his knee with a squeaky-clean pair of low-cut kicks and a distressed orange T-shirt with the words Made in 1988 on it. The T-shirt, one of Jus' Flexx's latest, looked soft and worn like he'd had it forever.

He put a pencil behind his ear, playing the part of our floor supervisor to the max.

"All right." He pointed to the wall. "Kara's on accessory and shoe duty. At least if you get all the heels shining, nobody will notice when a celeb's dogs are barking."

Me and Chandra barked, a roo, roo, roo. Kara rolled her eyes. I swear it was easier for her to be fake annoyed than play along.

"I don't see how four-hundred-dollar shoes can still make your feet hurt," Chandra said, shaking her head.

Me and Kara both said at the same time, "Beauty is pain."

"Ay, jinx," Justice said.

"Buy me a Coke," I finished.

Kara chuckled. "Nope. You buy me a Coke, Princess."

Inside, I blanched at the name even though it felt like, maybe, a joke. No smoke detected. I smiled and she didn't roll her eyes. Something like happiness floated up to my head.

"Okay," Justice said, all business again. "So, Mari's checking inventory." He tipped the clipboard at me. I raised the roof, happy to avoid the job none of us wanted as he announced, "And on steamer duty—"

It wasn't like he was going to give the job to himself, but Kara beat on the table for a drumroll. I joined in, patting my legs. He let the "drama" build a few more seconds, then went, "Woomp woomp, sorry, Chandra. You're steaming and I'll hit the Style floor as the runner."

Chandra's tiny shoulders hitched as she turned to prepare her station.

"No sense in me even being upset. We all have to do it."

"Facts. That's how you ride," Justice said. He and Chandra knocked fists. "Maybe if we get done early, the twins will let us go."

"If Marques and Joel ever heard you call them that . . . ," I said, leaving the consequences to their imagination.

"Not like they'd hear us way down here," Kara said. Her eyebrow peaked. "Unless you plan on diming."

"No plans at all," I said, breezy while my temples boomed like a heartbeat.

Chandra broke in, chattering through the tension.

"Speaking of ending early. What y'all doing tonight?" She placed three racks within her reach. The clothes hung, limp and wrinkled, waiting for their moment with the steamer. "If I show up home too early my mother be trying to get me to come put in a few hours over at Bradley." She made a face. "I need plans."

I stayed quiet, letting the moment pass. We'd been together all week. I needed a break.

When no one bit, she went back to putting clothes in order. I think her feelings were hurt. And somebody should have said something. It just wasn't going to be me.

Kara to the rescue.

"Not gonna lie, but we already together all day," she said, letting us fill in the blank.

The silent rejection hung in the air until Justice said, "All right, I'm out." He pulled the canvas cart from its parking spot and made his way to the door.

I waited for Chandra to push and ask what I was doing for the weekend. But I guess three strikes was too much. The steamer hissed its readiness and she went to work.

I had a system. Wait until there were at least six items to put away. I didn't have anything to do for a while. Chandra and Kara were focused on their boring, tedious, but mandatory jobs.

Chandra moved all her blouses to the front, all dresses to one rack, and pants to another. It didn't make things move any faster, but everybody had their own system for getting the job done.

I jumped on the Buzz, checking out the few pics Rachel had put up from Camp Run 'Em to Death and Sammie's periodic rants about rude Burger Haven customers. I don't know how she was finding time to post. Or maybe the question was—how was she finding time to work?

I zinged her pic of a crusted-over ketchup bottle and commented: Eww. Hope you plan on cleaning that before I roll through tomorrow

Clearly as bored as I was, she @ed me, quick:

TFW your baby cousin @Mari_Golden got a better summer job than you. But I love her anteways

I laughed at the GIF of some curly hair dude smashing his computer's monitor on the ground.

I peeped up, to make sure Chandra hadn't magically steamed a whole rack while I was dazing. She had two blouses done and was as meticulous with the steaming as she'd been checking inventory. Based on how often she went over a piece before racking it, it was going to be a minute.

I glanced over to Kara. She lined up ten pairs of shoes, inspecting each. She placed some on one end of the table, others at the opposite end. For somebody who rarely said a kind word, she surprised me with how okay she seemed with the chores.

I checked out her outfit. She had on a pair of skinny jeans with rips and tears in all the right places—the knee, small patch on the thigh, little shred on the shin. A red bandeau was visible from the sides of her Snoopy tee shirt that had been DIYed—sleeves cut then banded together in a makeshift twist knot down her back. Her accessories gave the outfit that Holly touch—gigantic hoop earrings in two of her holes and a ruby in the third. The lip gloss was popping again, a burnt red instead of pink.

Every time I looked at her, I wanted to tell her to chill with some of the overkill. I knew better. She wasn't down with me like that.

Another check had Chandra at four items. I was ready to blow off my so-called system just so I could get up and move around when Kara lined up ten more pairs of shoes then separated them. Curiosity got the best of me.

"What are you dividing them based on?"

She pointed to the shoes farthest from her. "Those all need a damage report." She picked up a pair of strappy sandals. "These just need to be cleaned and tagged."

"Makes it go by faster," I said, impressed. On my day as shoe mule, I'd taken one pair at a time, cleaned or tagged them.

"If you can call it faster. It still take all day," Kara said with a sigh.

"True that," I muttered.

When she wasn't scowling, her entire face changed. Wipe down some of that lip gloss and lose the huge earrings and she could have even been a private school chick. She was cute and I wondered if Justice thought so. Was he downplaying me so Kara wouldn't think I was his girlfriend?

"Has anybody else noticed that it's always the same amount of shoes each day," she asked. She shook a striped canvas slip-on at the cart of shoes. "For real, I wonder if somebody don't just dump shoes in here so we have something to do."

"That would be so messed up," Chandra said, never looking away from the dress she was tackling. A puff of steam went up.

"I don't think they'd do that," I said, even though in the back of my mind I couldn't say it was impossible. M & J obviously wanted to keep us busy so they could do their own thing in the afternoons. I defended Flexx instinctively. "Between the style clients, the magazine, and the Flexx TV shows they go through a lot of inventory. It's probably all legit."

Kara looked at the growing mountain of shoes, seemed to consider it, then shrugged.

Justice wheeled through, earbuds in, softly rapping as he went to empty the cart. The lyrics floated our way before he disappeared to the back.

"'Rising Son,'" I said, calling out the song he'd been rapping.

Kara nodded. "'Check the Game.' That's my track."

"Mine too," I said.

Chandra raised her hand. "Me too."

I felt like throwing my arms open and announcing, Hey, we all agreed on something. I kept myself in check and hollered over to Justice as he headed back out, "You sure you don't need help. Chandra gonna be a while."

Chandra opened her mouth to defend herself, saw the big cheese on my face, and giggled.

"Y'all know me. This better . . ."

"Than cleaning toilets," all three of us said.

Our laughter brightened up the cave's drabness.

Justice wheeled his cart over, leaning on it. "I think I just saw CoCo Blue."

"Probably true, Joel said she's the fall cover for *Flexx Mag*," Chandra said, head bobbing.

"The phat-phat is juicy in real life as it is on TV," Justice said, head shaking like he was reliving the sighting.

"Okay, gross. Bye," I said, shooing him away.

"Wow, you gon' say that right in front of your girlfriend," Kara said. "No respect."

"She's not my girlfriend," Justice said, easing his buds back into his ears.

The air in my lungs burned as Kara's eyebrow peaked. A smile played on her lips.

Here we go, I thought. I swiveled my stool back and forth, pretending to be fascinated with the notices about safety and inventory control on the nearby wall. I'd never been so happy to hear Chandra's voice as I was when she said, "Mari, are you ever going to accept my Buzz request?" She put up one hand, cross guarding my response. "You know how people are. If it's not on the Buzz it didn't happen. People don't believe I work with you."

She laughed, not quite embarrassed but maybe surprised that she'd said what she'd obviously been feeling all week. Before I could answer, Kara snorted.

"She probably need whoever works her social accounts to approve it."

I answered the question Chandra's widened eyes were asking. "I do my own social media." I grabbed my phone, opening it to the long list of unanswered requests, mostly people at school who I wouldn't accept if they paid me. "I'm just really bad at keeping up with requests."

I flashed the flooded screen of dark blue unconfirmed requests at her.

I could always unfollow her after summer was over. I clicked accept. "We official, now."

"Well all right," she said, smiling big. She went back to steaming, her spirits high enough that she started humming.

Kara was always so quick to instigate. I flipped things on her.

"How come you ain't request me, Kara?"

She put a pair of red stilettos on the table. "'Cause I can follow who I want. And I'm not like you. I'm not gon' add somebody just 'cause I feel bad that they trolling for a request."

Chandra pouted. "I wasn't trolling."

Kara didn't pay her any mind. An icy smile spread on her face. "What? You gon' run and tell Marques and Joel I'm not your Buzz friend?"

She turned her back and wiped down the stilettos, like she knew I wouldn't answer.

I stood up, took two steps closer to her so I didn't have to talk too loud. Not that I could. My mouth was the Sahara.

Chandra had the steamer up, frozen in place, watching. Puffs of mist blew our way. They died before they reached the six feet separating us.

"Kara, look . . ."

She turned, an expectant smirk on her face. The red

stiletto hung from the crook of her finger, swinging back and forth like a pendulum counting down to the drama I'd brought on myself.

My tongue clicked as I talked.

"It's not like we have to be best friends." That sounded silly out loud and worse, like that's what I wanted from her. Hardly. I was just tired of the salt. It brought all of my mother out of me, like she'd jumped into my body and took over my mouth. "But we gonna be together a few weeks. We should probably get to know each other instead of always dissing."

I couldn't see how anybody could argue with that. But this was Kara.

"I already know you," she said. The shoe fell to the table with a clunk as she used her fingers to count down the ways. "You in DC Magazine once a year as the 'first family' of hip-hop fashion." She rolled her eyes. "You go to Flowered Arms. You medaled in the 100 and 400 last spring. Your favorite color is orange . . . at least it was last year. You and Justice basically the only two Black people in your grade, so probably everybody think y'all boyfriend and girlfriend . . . but obviously you not." Her arms folded against her chest so tight that a bit of cleavage rose in the homemade V neck of her T-shirt, brown mounds behind Snoopy's ears. "What I'm missing?"

My face burned. The only thing worse than being dragged was being dragged with things that are true. Kara knew I had already taken my best shot.

"I thought so," she said. She picked up the heels and began wiping them down with an alcohol pad. "Look, take it how you want. We work together. That don't make us friends. I'm cool with that." She looked over at me, making sure I was listening. "You need to be, too."

She made a tag for the heels, then walked past me toward the cart of shoes. Our arms brushed as she passed. Hers were ice cold. My head knew it was because the storeroom stayed chilly. My heart felt like it was because she was such a witch. Her goose bumps infected my hot skin and I broke out in my own set.

I grabbed the clothes Chandra had steamed so far and disappeared to the back of the cave, avoiding the silent apology Chandra sent with her eyes.

Her pity made my stomach churn.

If I had walked away any faster I would have been running.

CHAPTER .15.

Loyalty is funny.

Not ha ha funny. Complicated funny.

Real deal, how many people can you really be down for?

I didn't want to tell Sammie how Justice had carried me all week. How it felt like him and Kara were talking mess about me. Shoot, I didn't want to believe he was doing that. But there wasn't no other way to call it.

I was desperate when I texted:

Justice tripping so hard right now

She hit right back:

What he do?

And I told her. As sweet as it was to finally tell somebody

else how lonely I'd been all week, how invisible I felt—I regretted it immediately.

I managed to stop her from dragging him into our chat so she could "Let him be real about it." I even got her to promise that she wouldn't say anything on Saturday, unless I gave her the code word—onions.

I hated onions. But if I asked for onions on my burger, she had my permission to step to him.

My stomach was bubbly. I almost wanted to give Justice a heads-up. But that loyalty thing had me twisted. I prayed that me and Jus had a chance to talk. Maybe I was the one tripping. Maybe work-Justice was kind of wack but would be off for the weekend.

I picked out a pink puffed-sleeve cotton dress. It reminded me of the smocks we got in art class but with a fashion remix. The neck was square, the body flared and higher in the front than the back. Then the sleeves had a girly swell to them, like I had a half-inflated balloon on each arm. I hooked it up with a pair of all-white tennas and went hunting for Mommy.

She was in the sunroom, her favorite part of the house.

It looked out into our small backyard, which was surrounded by a thicket of trees that made the next block of houses feel farther away than they were. The entire room was enclosed by glass and wooden beams, and the brown tile was like fancy dirt. The glass ceiling even had real ivy around the beams to make it feel like you were in a little hideaway among the trees. Mommy called it bringing the outside in.

She was stretched out on her wicker chaise, twirling a piece of hair around her finger, head cocked quizzically at the book she was reading. I sat cross-legged in one of the chairs in the corner across from her and waited patiently for her to take a break.

I stared at the wall of trees in awe that a whole loud city was out there behind the capsule of green. No one would ever know it in the quiet sunroom.

My mother's voice jolted me. "What are you so dressed up for?"

In public, Mommy's clothes were always deliberate. But in the house, she was definitely an athleisure, fun-T-shirt-wearing person. Even when me and Daddy dressed down we were dressed up.

"I mean, it's not dressed up for me," I said, standing up to give her a model twirl.

"Are you still meeting Sammie at the Haven?" I nodded and she laughed. "Even for you, that's a little fancy. But I dig. I dig. You cute, too."

I chuckled at how much she sounded like Daddy. "Thank ya. Thank ya," I said, sitting on the edge of the chaise.

She scooted her feet over, then placed the book on her lap. I felt the Cee Oh Oh coming in the way she took a breath before saying, "I had a good talk with Marques yesterday." Even with her pause welcoming me to say something, I stayed quiet, smart enough to let her go first so I knew how to respond. "He said that you all are doing well. Taking the fashion history as serious as the fun stuff."

I stretched my eyes. "What's the fun stuff?"

"The games you all play." Her eyebrow peaked in challenge. "He and Joel put a lot of time into finding ways to teach you how to style without actually teaching, Marigold."

I hadn't thought about it like that. "True. No, the challenges are fun."

Her eyes brightened. "And they served a purpose. We have a big surprise coming for you all."

This time her pause worked. "What?" I asked.

"The VGAs are coming and this year we're going to let you all help style two clients." Her smile was all teeth at my surprised gasp. "Yep. We thought it would be nice if young stylists worked with young clients."

"Wait. You already know who we're going to style?"

Her head bobbed enthusiastically.

"Who?"

She picked up her book. "You'll see."

I stood up. "Ma, you can't do that. Whoooo?" I did a tiny tantrum stomp.

She laughed. "Magiq and STARZ. This is a big deal. You'll be guided closely by Marques and Joel, but we're excited to let you all have a real-life Flexx experience."

"Jus is going to wil' out."

"As he should," she said, making me laugh at how proper it sounded.

"Can I tell him, today?" The thought of us having a secret was it. It would make up for telling Sammie what I did.

Mommy frowned.

I clasped my hands and begged. "Please?"

Her lips tightened as she processed whether to give me what I wanted. "Okay, yes." She sighed. "And it's pointless of me to say this but I'll say it anyway—don't tell anyone else. We'd like for you all to be surprised. We want the energy to be a reward for the good work you've all done."

"I promise," I said, swiping her cheek with a hasty kiss. "Thank you, Mommy."

I was out of the house like I was on fire. There were only ten people on the Metro. As it went underground, I zoned out, bubbling on how Justice would take the VGA news.

The Van Gogh Awards was peak streets-is-talking kind of award. Artists who wanted to lay claim to being about the music, lyrics, and the culture wanted a Van Gogh. What made VGAs really buzzy is that artists could only receive it once. Which was enough. Performers blew up, after. VGAs had made and revived a lot of hip-hop careers.

And the panel was super secret. Instead of nomination announcements, artists received an invitation with writing in legit gold leaf two weeks before the show.

Justice and the crew were going to get the real real on Flexx over the next two weeks—client interviews, consults, and fittings. And we'd get to be in on them instead of walking by on our way to the storeroom.

The wheels of the Metro squealed as the canned voice announced Turner Avenue. Marks Parks was a nabe of short cottage-looking houses. Every single one had two large windows that took up the front of the house and only enough grass to be a nuisance. It was easy to see who had been in Marks for years and who was new-ish. The OGs's fronts were dusty red brick. The nubes had nice, new siding, screaming, Look at me! Everybody had their space enclosed by a wire fence, protecting their tiny piece of land. Ms. Sadie's house tricked you. She was an OG but Daddy had talked her into renovating—hoping she'd sell it, but no go.

I slowed down as I walked past her tidy yard. The white siding was so bright it seemed to gleam in the sun. Two metal rockers, missing their cushions, sat on her front porch. Memories of Ms. Sadie watching me and Sammie play tag made my heart happy sad. The house looked lonely. I think it missed us.

As soon as I turned the block, I saw Justice and Spank, his best friend, sitting on his front stoop. Since when was Spank invited?

I swallowed the saltiness in my throat.

"'Bout time, girl. What took so long?" Spank asked, already up and walking toward me signaling my answer didn't matter.

"If I knew y'all were waiting, I could have met y'all there," I said, as my little legs hustled to keep up with their long ones.

"That's what I said." Spank rolled his eyes. His phone chirped. He lost himself in a text message.

Me and Spank had only seen each other a few times.

He wasn't unfriendly but I still wasn't sure if he liked me.

"I didn't know I was tagging along all in y'all plans," I said more to Justice than Spank, this time.

Justice mimed shooting a basketball. "Naw, that's on me. Spank stopped by and I figured it was cool if he rolled through to Haven with us. Is it?"

He knew I wasn't going to say no. Not in front of Spank, at least. I nodded, then clamped my mouth shut and kept my head down, letting the flow of my feet calm me. My dress swayed around my legs, a tiny ripple of pink. My white tennas peeked out with each step. Pink wave, white peek, pink wave, white peek until I wasn't mad anymore.

Marks was busier than T-Hill. People were already hanging out in their front yards, kids were playing, cars were being washed, music came from porches or open windows. I talked over the noise.

"I'm just glad to get out of the house. Weekends are so boring."

Spank looked up long enough to say, "Where you live, maybe."

"Thanks, Spank, for confirming my nabe is wack," I said, knowing he was right.

For sure, T-Hill wasn't like the Black neighborhoods

where most everybody went to whatever school was in that area. In the Hill a lot of us went to different private schools. I barely knew some of the kids on my block. And even if I had close friends there, people in nabes like mine were usually ghost the entire summer.

We got inside the station just as the Metro pulled up. The train was standing-room only. Spank leaned against the wall in a spot reserved for wheelchairs. Justice and I stood by one pole, his hand above mine, the other on my waist. He was only doing it because we were squeezed together so tightly. I didn't hate it.

I wanted to mention the VGAs but the Metro was loud and it felt funny talking about Style High around Spank. He probably didn't want to hear about it. Justice steadied me as the train jerked.

"For real, I thought you was gonna invite Chandra to kick it today," he said, talking down toward my ear.

I gripped the pole tighter as the train shuddered, squinting up at him. "Why would I do that?"

"Seemed like y'all getting closer." He shrugged. "Plus, we had moves already, wouldn't have mattered to me if you tagged her in."

Key word, we had plans, Justice.

"You could have invited her," I said, not meaning it. "I

definitely would make sure Sammie knew it was your idea to roll through her job mob deep."

"Oh, true. I can see her now—Who all these people?" His hand gripped my waist as the Metro halted. We lurched. I held on to the pole for dear life then sank against him when we moved again.

Sammie might do that anyway when he showed up with Spank. I'd let him fight that battle when we crossed that bridge.

Since he'd brought up Chandra, I let go of the pole and leaned my back against it, so I could look him in the eye. He hunched over, leaning his head near my mouth to hear me over the robotic announcement of the next station. "All right, I know Kara was just trying to start stuff yesterday by calling me your girlfriend." I gave him a chance to react. He stayed in listening mode. "But you played me off so fast. It was like you couldn't wait to set it straight."

He straightened up, eyes focused ahead of him. "Okay, but we not together like that. I figured you'd want everybody to know the real."

"I mean . . . I do. I—"

"And keeping it a stack, I don't want nobody thinking I only got into Style High because we friends." He raised an eyebrow at me. "They really gonna believe that if they think we a couple."

I hadn't thought about it like that. Justice probably saw it in my face. I braced myself for him to go in on me about privilege blah, blah. The conductor saved me, announcing U Street and telling us to have a pleasant weekend.

"This us," Spank said, like we hadn't heard the same announcement. Closest to the doors, he was out in seconds, in his own world as he followed the crowd above ground.

Justice guided me through the bodies, keeping his hand on the small of my back. He didn't say anything until we were outside. Spank was on the phone now, five steps ahead of us, telling somebody about a party popping off later.

Justice slowed his pace. "I don't want you mad at me. It'll be bad for my career." As I opened my mouth to say something he laughed. "I'm joking, Mari. I know you and Kara got some smoke between you, but she all right with me. Can't we just ride it out the next few weeks?"

"I don't have no smoke with Kara, for your information," I said. He didn't attempt to speak for whether Kara had smoke with me and I was too afraid to ask. I shrugged so hard it tweaked my shoulder. "But it's all good. I can ride it out."

He laced me with one of those smiles that made the girls all fluttery. I shoved him in the chest like I was exasperated to keep myself from hugging him. I hadn't felt this close to him all week.

The city was alive. Music pumped out of something called Bistro Bally's. It was new to me. Despite us coming back for church services, I hadn't been to this block since last summer. I gazed into Bally's window as we went by. A small band was on a smaller stage right in front of the window. It made me want to stop and listen, join the crowd of people doing the same. I let myself be pulled along past a few more places, smelling of Indian food, then Korean, then beer.

The air was hot and humid, but bearable as the sun periodically dipped behind fluffy clouds. No one seemed in a hurry to be anywhere. I guess they, like us, were all already where they wanted to be, too.

The line to Burger Haven was wrapped half a block back. Some people had that all-day lean, against meters, trees, trash cans, whatever they found along the way to hold their weight. The smell of fresh ground beef sizzled out of the door and hung in the air. It was why no one had given up on the line.

My mouth watered already, thinking about a burger

oozing with American cheese on a warm sesame bun.

"We gonna be here a minute," Spank said, disappointed.

I tugged Justice—"Naw. Sammie got us"—and headed down an alley before anyone objected. Alleys reminded me of dark and filth, but Sammie had told me what to do.

I was relieved that the alley was short. It smelled like old grease and was littered with stacks of boxes labeled USDA Prime, but it seemed almost clean. Sammie stood at the back of the Haven, waiting. Justice and Spank exchanged pounds, slapping hands then touching knuckles.

Her locs were pulled back, held together by a thick black band that blended into her hair. Usually styled out in rompers, she looked plain and unremarkable in her work uniform, a pair of fitted jeans, hugged to her thick waist by a belt, and a black T-shirt with sandwich buns outlined in white. In red, gold, white, and green, the words ketchup, mayo, onions, and lettuce floated in between the buns.

"Heyy," I sang.

"What up, boo?" Sammie said. She squinted at Spank like she was trying to figure out who or what he was.

Justice spoke up. "You be able to hook Spank up too? He rolled through last-minute."

Sammie's face said she didn't believe it. She groused at him. "Yeah, but he taking your burger. How 'bout that?"

"Don't do me like that," Justice said with that smile.

Sammie took a small pad out of the back of her pocket, removed a pencil hidden in her hair.

"Tell me what y'all want. I'm gonna get it cooked and then take it with me once I clock out."

"This won't get you in trouble, will it?" I asked.

I looked around. The only movement in the alley was a wrapper skittering through, trying to make its way out.

"I'm getting y'all hamburgers, not drugs," she said with a laugh. "Relax. I get free food as long as I order while I'm on the clock."

Justice and Spank obeyed, placing their orders. All three of them looked at me. Her pencil frozen above the pad, Sammie prodded me. "You eating too? Please don't tell me you becoming one of them chicks who don't like eating anything around dudes but salad."

"Please. You know I will mess up a burger. I don't care who's around," I said, making the guys laugh.

Spank put his meaty hand out and I tapped it, feeling ridiculously feminine beside him.

I gave her my order.

"Did you want onions?" she asked, her eyes sliding quickly to the left where Justice stood. Too quick for anybody but me to catch, probably.

"Nope. I'm good," I said, feeling the weight of the almost confrontation slide away.

She nodded, eyes roaming the list one more time. Assured it was right, the pad disappeared back into her pocket, the pencil into the mass of hair. "All right. I meet y'all at Mac Park in like fifteen minutes," she said before disappearing back inside.

CHAPTER .16

Mac Park, short for MacArthur, was a recreation park two blocks away. As we walked from the Haven, people on the prowl for Saturday-night plans gave way to fitness buffs getting in late afternoon jogs and families trying to wear the kids out. The massive park stretched out in front of us, treeless, all playgrounds, baseball fields, basketball courts, and jogging trails.

Spank took a break from his phone and walked in step with me and Justice.

"Ay, so baby girl you told me about still meeting us?" he asked. His eyes shone with anticipation.

"Yeah, probably," Justice mumbled.

"She bringing a friend?" Spank asked.

"Ioun even know," Justice said.

"I hope so," Spank said, and swear to God rubbed his hands together like somebody who couldn't wait to tear open a gift. "Reece said he know her from the Holly community center. Said she that bait. You know pretty girls always run in cliques."

Justice shrugged, unwilling to discuss "baby girl's" hotness, and picked up his pace a few steps. It was obvious that he wanted to keep the conversation as short as possible. Which is exactly why I piped in.

"Who's baby girl?"

I walked double-time to pace with his new stride.

"Kara," Justice said, cutting his eyes at Spank.

Spank got the message and lagged behind. He jumped on the phone again, shouting out plans to someone. Mr. Party Planner.

The pounding was either my heartbeat or my stomping feet. I snapped. "You invited Kara to hang out with us? Why?"

Justice jammed his hands into his pockets. It seemed to slow his pace. Or maybe he knew he couldn't outrun the conversation. His shoulders went up to his ears, came down hard in a shrug.

"She wasn't doing nothing today, okay? When she

asked what the moves were, I told her."

"That's why you wanted me to ask Chandra? So it wouldn't look as foul that you invited Kara?"

"Foul? Wow. It's foul that I invited her?" He put his hand up like I was physically fighting him. "First of all, Kara just hit me up a few hours ago. And it's a free country, Mari. Anybody can come to Mac Park. You know that, right?"

"Yeah, I know that, Justice, thanks," I shot back.

"It's not like I brought her to Burger Haven with us. I knew Sammie would trip if we added another burger to the order." He raised his arms, let them fall to his sides. "She just wanna kick it. That's all."

His attitude annoyed me. Made me feel like I was wrong. Like I should feel bad for being mad that he invited every person he met to just "kick it." How was I being petty for wanting time with him without his other friends around?

Thinking about Kara being his friend sat in my throat hard and immovable.

We walked the rest of the way, silent.

At one point his arm brushed against mine. An apology, maybe. I took a step away.

About ten feet into the park, I spotted Kara.

She was hard to miss. She was the only person sitting alone near a baseball field. She was perched on top of a faded wooden picnic table, wearing orange short-shorts and a fitted tank top that hugged her every curve, talking on her phone. Her weave was out, hanging to the middle of her back.

As Justice scanned the area, searching, I begrudgingly pointed her out.

"That's probably her."

"Oh, all right," he said. He brushed against me again. "Thanks."

A look passed between us. His version of an apology. I looked away. This wasn't okay. If he'd just told me he'd invited her, it would have been different. Maybe.

Not really.

Anger built in my head like a swarm of flies on rotting meat—hungry and chaotic.

When we were still a good twenty feet away Kara waved us over.

"Ay, let me call you back. My people here," she said into the phone. "All right. Yeah, all right . . ." She clamped her fingers together to show us the person wouldn't shut up. "Myra, all right, damn. I call you later. Okay. See you." She stood up on the table's bench seat and stretched like she'd been there awhile. She pulled at the shorts. What good it did. They came down maybe a centimeter.

Beside me, Spank eyed every inch of her leg. I wondered if he was the only one enjoying the show, but I resisted the urge to peek at Justice.

Kara blessed Spank with a smile. My presence didn't seem to surprise her at all. Of course. She'd known about the plans.

Justice gave her a nod, then sat on the table's edge, next to her. At least he wasn't standing there staring all into her cooch.

He nudged her thigh with his elbow. "Mook said y'all supposed to hook up later."

Kara laughed up at the sky.

"Mook might wish that. But no." She eyed Spank good and hard. "I'm Kara, since Mari and Justice not trying introduce."

"My bad." Justice waved over in Spank's general direction. "This my boy, Spencer. We call him Spank."

She spoke with a playful song in her voice. "Hey, Spank."

"How you doing?" he said with this huge cat-ate-the-canary grin. He even put his hand out and she shook it, held on to it while she stepped down from the table, then sat down on the bench.

I sat on the bench seat, below where Justice perched. Spank walked around to the other side of the table, sat opposite Kara.

"Mari, look at you, out with the fellas," she said. With a casual cross of her legs, she talked across Justice toward me like we were old friends. "I figured you'd be out boating, jet skiing on the lake or whatever people on T-Hill do on the weekends."

Spank snorted. "Haa—"

"Man, shut up," Justice interrupted.

Not quite apologizing, Spank giggled. "Come on, yo, boating? Mari, your peoples got a boat?"

"No. But why is that so funny?" I asked, not caring anymore if he liked me or not. "Now, if I said it was funny 'cause you hang out on the street corner all day, I'd be wrong. Right?"

Spank's eyes were wide in his face and he didn't blink the next twenty seconds.

Kara cracked up. "Oorp, she went there."

"All right, y'all," Justice said. His thumb worked at his eyebrows. He looked out at the deserted field, refusing to look at any of us.

Even though I was on my own, against Kara, it didn't feel as scary. Mac Park was neutral ground. I didn't have to worry about "ruining" anybody's experience.

"So how come you didn't already have plans? No parties at the Rec tonight?" I asked, liking the sarcasm that dripped off my tongue, not caring if I was stereotyping.

Her eyebrow rose, but she only paused a second. For some reason giving me a pass rather than biting back like she normally did.

"Me and my friend Myra were supposed to kick it. But her crazy butt gets in trouble last night." She shook her head and sighed. "Justice said he was heading to Haven, so I told him scoop me up something. So—" She threw her hands in the air, let them smack her thighs. "Here I am. And now it's a Style High reunion. Somebody call Chandra."

Her cackle floated toward the empty field.

"Oh, my bad, I couldn't get you a burger," Justice said.

Kara scowled at him. "Boy, why not?"

Justice looked from me to her. "For real, I thought we were going inside, but Mari's cousin hooked us up on the low. You can have mine though."

I choked back a grunt. Note to self, never hook up Justice again.

"Oh, that's bet," she said, satisfied.

I envied how fast she got over being mad at him. What

was it about girls that we never did that with each other?

My phone rang. It was Sammie. "Hey. Yeah . . ." I stood up, swiveled to the right then left. "I don't see you." I half turned to the right again, put my hands up to my face, shielding nothing since the sun wasn't that bright, then waved. "Oh, see me? I'm waving. Yeah, next to the girl with the orange shorts. Okay."

Samej strode over to the table. She placed a big brown paper bag in the middle of the table with a thump like a hood delivery girl.

"Those some heavy burgers," Spank said.

"Good, too. San hooked 'em up," she said, slightly winded. She sat down beside me, her back to the bag. When no one moved, she frowned. "I know y'all don't think I'm gonna dig in there and tell you whose sandwich is whose."

It was all the signal Spank needed. He lit into the bag.

"Samej, this is Kara," Justice said. "She in Style High with me and Mari."

Sammie looked at me at the same time Spank handed me my burger.

"Hey," Kara said, friendlier than I'd ever heard her talk to anybody besides Justice.

"Hey," Sammie said, flat.

Justice cut his burger in half and shared it with Kara. As everybody ate in silence for a few minutes, savoring the goodness of Burger Haven, I unwrapped my burger then muttered, "Shoot."

"What's wrong?" Justice asked.

"It's fine. I forgot to get onions, though," I said. I kept my eyes on my burger as Sammie tensed up next to me.

She jumped to her feet, stretched like she'd been sitting a long time, then asked casually, "Y'all work at Flexx with my auntie, huh?"

Kara plucked a pickle off the burger and threw it on the grass. Her mouth crimped in question. "Who's your aunt?"

I answered, hoping by talking I'd blow away the nerves building. "Sammie's father and my mother are brother and sister."

"Why you not in the program then?" Spank asked. "Shoot, if I had a rich uncle I wouldn't be flipping no burgers."

Sammie folded her arms. "A, I'm in tenth grade. That's too old for Style High. B, even if I was, fashion not my thing." She talked to him like he was five years old. "C, my aunt is the rich one, thank you very much, and D, I'm on my own grind. Don't knock the hustle."

Spank put his hands up like he was being jacked. "My bad. My bad."

Kara chuckled. "She dragged you, though."

"Plus, for real, I'm not down with people acting different just 'cause they got put on," Sammie said, still in Spank's direction.

My breath caught as Justice looked up, eyebrows frowning.

"Ioun know nothing about that," Spank said, finishing off his burger and wiping his mouth.

"Justice might," Sammie said, hands on her hip.

Justice looked to Sammie then me. "I'm acting different?" he asked, his voice high. "How I'm acting different?"

I wanted to jump in but Sammie was on it. "Why you treating Mari like you barely know her? She be having your back all the time up at that school. Now you doing her dirty."

Justice popped off the bench. "I don't know what Mari been telling you but I ain't doing nothing. And she the one who got 'put on.' She ain't even know about the program till I told her."

"Ayne," Spank said, covering his mouth with his fist.

Kara's eyes rolled. "How you ain't know about something

like that? You live right there in the house with the person who came up with the idea."

I defended myself. "Easy. My parents live in their world and I live in mine."

"If it's not about you, you on to the next, huh?" Kara said, never blinking as I scowled at her.

"I didn't say that." My voice was tight as I tried to keep a grip on my slipping temper.

"None of that even matter," Sammie said, unruffled by Kara. "But let me find out anybody dogging my baby cousin. Let it be on 'cause it will be."

"Dogging her?" Justice asked, looking at me.

His nose was flared in anger. But I saw the hurt in his eyes.

It was too late to explain why I'd sicced Sammie on him. There was no calling her back. I stayed silent, not wanting to make Sammie mad by flip-flopping. I'd have to explain to Justice later. Maybe after Kara left. I felt even more sick when she jumped in on his side.

"Mari, if you and Justice so close, why you ain't just say how you was feeling?" She shook her head like it was so obvious. Like she wasn't the reason I hadn't been able to talk to Justice all week. Her always being there. Him defending her whenever I pointed out how annoying she was.

"It's not even your business, for real," Sammie said.

Kara's head whipped Sammie's way. They glared at each other, feeling out the situation.

Sammie had two inches and twenty pounds on Kara. Still, Kara looked like she could handle her own. She didn't look scared of Sammie, only like she was weighing whether fighting was worth it.

Justice stood between them. "It ain't even that deep, Sammie."

"It can be," Kara said.

Sammie stared Kara down one good time, then snorted, "Hmmph."

Spank stood up on the bench. "All right. All right. Ain't nobody trying referee no fight. It's too hot for all that."

"Facts," Kara said. She made a face, bored with the conversation. "What else popping tonight?"

"Party at 13th and N," Spank announced, proudly promoting like he was making a cut from the event.

"What time?" Justice asked. He pulled out his cell, checked the time. "I need go home and shower first."

"Nine," Spank said. "We trying roll through?"

I sat silent as they made the plans around me, like I wasn't there. Sammie perched on the edge of the table, texting.

"I don't think I know nobody out on 13th. Friendlies or what?" Justice asked. He took it upon himself to gather the little balls of foil that had held the burgers and dump them into the empty bag.

"Mos def. I'm down with the 13th Ave crew. It's good," Spank said.

"I'm going," Kara said. "Justice, can you stop with me to my house so I can change?"

"Man, who got time for all that?" Spank said.

"Today? You do," Kara said, poking him in the chest. "Come on. If we leave now, it's plenty of time."

She stood up. Tugged at the shorts. Spank sucked his teeth. It was for show, though. He got up, ready to follow her on command.

"You going, Mari?" Kara asked, voice sweet, face skeptical.

Sammie rolled her eyes, but kept her face on her phone.

"I'm good," I said.

I looked over at Justice, trying to apologize with my eyes.

His eyes skated away. "Ay, thanks for the burgers, Sammie."

"Umhm," she said, not bothering to look up. "You welcome."

Justice shook his head. "All right, well, we out. Talk to you later, Marigold."

"See you, Mari," Spank said, already walking away.

Justice and Kara turned and followed him. When they were only a few feet away her laughter drifted back loud and mocking, like either Justice had said something funny or she had.

Sammie looked after them. "Don't even stunt that. He tripping 'cause he got a little crush."

I knew that was supposed to make me feel better. It didn't.

CHAPTER .17.

YES!

I reread Chandra's message. My fingers trembled a little as I sent her a smiley face emoji.

Maybe I was digging a brand-new hole for myself but I couldn't play sick and I couldn't walk into Flexx with Justice mad at me and teamed with Kara. I needed a friendly face. Even if Chandra was only being friendly because she was afraid she'd get kicked out the program, I'd take it. I had to.

I texted her and asked if we could meet at Java's, a coffee shop in the Ryder Station Metro stop, and her message came back so fast I half expected her to be standing there when I looked up from the screen.

I almost told her why I was randomly hitting her up but couldn't risk screenshot shenanigans. I waited until after we had our drinks to fill her in on the weekend.

Chandra sipped her frozen latte, hummed with pleasure, then picked up where she left off. "Don't take this the wrong way, okay?" Her brown eyes were solemn. She legit waited for me to say, "Okay," before she went on. "You're too pressed."

My mouth hovered above my straw. I frowned at her. "Is there really any good way for me to take that?"

Chandra laughed. "Probably not. Just saying that Justice on his grind this summer. Not to say that he shouldn't be able to do that and still rock with y'all friendship, but . . ." She slurped. "I don't know. But if you keep pushing it's probably only going to get worse."

"I think it's already worse," I said, feeling the truth in her words in the pit of my stomach.

"You did call your cousin in on him, though." Her skinny shoulder shrugged.

I'd been too honest with her. It smacked me in the face. Chandra backpedaled, probably with thoughts of her spot in the program on her mind. "But he shoulda had more respect for y'all friendship. He could have at least told you he invited Kara."

"Right?" I said, latching onto anything that sided with me.

I licked at the whipped cream on my frappé. The sugar melted on my tongue and into my bloodstream, making me feel more awake.

Chandra's hair was in two big braids. She pulled at one absently.

"You think him and Kara talking?" she asked.

"I don't know. For real, sometimes it feels like he's mad at me because I remind him of school," I said. My drink was forgotten as I thought about it. "I think he's mad I'm here, but not like he's going to say that."

She nodded. "He better not."

She laughed as she sucked on her drink. A few commuters looked over, mildly concerned, at the young girl choking. I'm sure somebody would have helped if Chandra hadn't been laughing just as hard as she was hacking. I tapped her back. It didn't do much. She hacked one last time before getting it together.

"I mean, I get it. I can't wait to get away from Bradley. But you not like them. I don't see why it should matter to Justice that you're here. You been cool."

The round lights on the platform blinked fast. My meek "Thanks" was lost as the train rushed into the station. Chandra was just boosting my ego. I didn't care. I needed it.

I broke out in goose bumps as the train swept by, spewing a cold breeze. It squealed to a stop. We hid our drinks in our bags and shuffled on board. Chandra easily slipped by a few people and stole a set of the bright orange seats as a woman was lowering herself into one of them.

Once the train pulled off, our drinks came back out. I pretended not to see the look of disapproval from the guy with a beard standing in front of us. He was totally profiling us, probably figured me and Chandra would leave our trash on our seats. He looked smack like my biology teacher except redder in the face, like he'd hustled for the train. I almost put my drink away, then realized this wasn't school. And no matter what Justice thought, I wasn't some Flo-A ghost haunting him. I slurped the last of my frappé, boldly staring at Bearded Guy until he turned his pinched face away.

My heart ticked crazily, excited and a little scared at the same time. I was usually "book in face girl" on the train or "admiring the cityscape chick."

"Look at you, got a little rebel in you," Chandra said, giggling.

"Very little," I said. I dropped my cup back into my

bag. Bearded Guy noted from the side of his eyes. I sniffed in satisfaction that we'd disappointed him. "Anyway, I sent him a text apologizing, asking if we could talk, but he never hit me back."

"So he big mad," Chandra said.

Dread sat in my chest as I nodded.

"For real, he'll get over it."

"I guess," I said, unconvinced.

Our stop was next. She stood up. "Look, he better. Being mad at you not gonna get him very far at Flexx."

The words rang in my ears. A five-alarm fire reminding me that I really wasn't one of them. Wasn't one of anybody.

I stayed seated. Chandra put her bag on her seat, held on to the pole to steady herself against the train's motion. We were silent for a few seconds until she said, "Oh, guess what I heard?"

"What?" I asked half-heartedly.

"I think we gonna get to help style for the VGAs." Her smile was a mile wide. "If that happens, oh my God, it will be the dopest thing I have ever done in my life."

I stood up, grabbing the pole. "Who you hear that from?"

"Kara dropped it in the group chat. She said she overheard Marques and Joel talking." Almost shyly, she asked, "Is it true?"

If I said yes, it would only prove I knew stuff the others didn't. Things I obviously wasn't sharing. I went with a shrug and muttered, "I don't know." Chandra chattered the rest of the way to the office, then squealed when we stepped into the Closet and saw that every style hub was occupied. Senior stylists were everywhere—gathered at the circulation desk, checking off orders, running from rack to rack.

I followed her gaze to the flat screens.

A monitor flashed the message: "It's Time! The VGAs are in 11 days, 11 hours, 5 minutes, 31 seconds."

"It's true," she said. She squeezed me tighter than I thought her tiny arms could. "Oh my God, it's true, Mari. I wonder who got an invite this year." She craned her neck to look back at the screen. There was no need. All the flat screens in the Closet had the same message. "Ooh I hope Lil' Mike got one. He's so cute."

Her excitement finally infected me. "I know for sure that we're styling Magiq and STARZ."

Her head shook in wonder. "You knew?"

"My mother told me Saturday. If things hadn't gone sideways, I was going to tell Justice but—" I shrugged, swallowing against the egg in my throat. For a second, it flashed that maybe it would have changed the vibe between me, Kara, and Justice if I had told them about the VGAs. It would have been nice that being the group's inside connect was a good thing.

Instead, I unleashed Sammie on him. In fifteen steps we would be at the hub. In fifteen steps I'd find out how he wanted to carry it from here. I was scared. But I also wanted to get it out of the way.

Chandra spilled over with questions.

Had I ever been to the VGAs? Yes.

What was it like? As cool as it seems.

How had a bunch of Pop Princesses like STARZ gotten an invite?

I only laughed. I felt the same way.

When we got to our desks, the first ones to our section, she put her pinky out.

"Promise you won't hold my stanning against me," she said dramatically.

I wanted to make her promise to have my back and not leave me lonely once Kara and Justice arrived. Instead, I laughed as I linked my pinky with hers and shook.

Justice came in right behind us.

"Hey," Chandra said extra loud.

"What's up?" Justice said, taking his seat.

"Hey," I said, forcing the words above a whisper and

thankful he hadn't only spoken to Chandra. Maybe it wasn't too bad. I sat in my seat, leg jiggling, as Chandra went on about the VGAs and wondering if we'd get to attend. Kara straggled in without a hello or a glance, seconds before Marques and Joel.

"I see everybody is back," Marques said, his smile thin. "No one mutinied over the weekend. Guess that means either we didn't give you enough prep work last week—"

"Or you really want to be here," Joel finished. His big cheeks expanded an inch or two as he beamed at us. "No one likes prep work. But it's part of the job. Even when you get to our level."

Marques gave him this look as if to say, Speak for yourself, before getting right to it.

"Unless you're clueless to the nth degree, you can see that the VGAs are coming. We're officially on the clock," Marques said. He consulted his tablet. I sat up straighter, looked around for the material for our challenge. Realized the cart wasn't out. "Flexx's roster of VGA guests grows every year. This year, we're styling five of the presenters, one of the MCs, and . . ." His finger flicked the screen. He smiled down at it, satisfied. "We're styling eight artists who received an invite. Lucky ducklings that you are, you'll get to play a part in this."

Joel went on. "Originally, you would have had nearly four weeks managing the storeroom—"

Kara snorted, a Puh, raising Marques's eyebrow.

"Something to share, Ms. Knight?" he asked.

"Managing the storeroom sound way more important than it is," she said, unshaken by the Marques eyebrow of doom.

"Well, somebody has to do it," Marques said. "And preparing for big events like VGAs will show you why." He humphed. "All right, Marigold and Kara, go with Joel." His gesture commanded us to move as he doled out more assignments.

"Good luck," Chandra exhaled softly beside me.

"You, too," I said, bending to get my bag.

Next thing I knew, me and Kara were sitting in Joel's cube. He sat behind his L-shaped desk in a chair that was too small for him. It wasn't a small chair, it was just too small for him.

He adjusted himself, finding what must have been his spot.

"I hope y'all understand what a big opportunity this is," he said, beaming sunshine at a thousand watts. "Not everybody is thrilled to babysit the trainees all summer." He dismissed that attitude with a wave. "But I'm excited to see what you all can do. I know a little about what Marigold can do." He raised an eyebrow at Kara. "But I don't know much about you, Miss Thing-Thing. But Marshall handpicked you, so that's all I need to know. He sees something in you."

My father, the forever savior of District City's "at-risk" kids.

Joel kept on through Kara's silence like it was normal to compliment somebody and have them say . . . absolutely nothing.

He leaned up and somehow his large belly fit under the desk. He handed us each a glossy photo. "Know who that is?"

Kara's nose wrinkled. "No. But he needs his hair cut."

Joel laughed. "From your lips to his ear, baby girl."

"It's Magiq," I said.

In the headshot Magiq was mean mugging. Kara pulled it closer to her face.

"I didn't picture him like this." She scowled at me, like I'd performed a trick. "How'd you know who it was?"

I shrugged. "Saw his pic on my father's desk one time. My parents talk about how to make Flexx the first place up-and-coming artists and entertainers make when they're ready to be styled."

"Magiq always spitting rhymes about not caring about

going mainstream. He don't even like being photographed," Kara said, still staring at the photo. Impressed for the first time.

I fed her quiet awe. "Yeah, I know. As soon as I saw the picture, I figured it was somebody that was probably ready to blow up."

"Yep. He's been on our radar for a while," Joel admitted.

Magiq was only sixteen, but he'd been grinding as an underground hip-hop artist for a few years. His mix tapes were fire. They popped up on random internet sites like a musical virus.

The old Kara returned. She frowned. "He looks homeless though."

Joel laughed good and hard. His belly shook against the keyboard, making it clink lightly.

"I'm surprised he's asking to be styled." He shrugged. "Maybe it's his 'people's' idea. Not really our concern. Just making him look good is."

"You think he's trying to get put on?" Kara asked, genuinely curious.

The fascination in her voice relaxed me.

"Everyone knows a VGA often leads to mainstream success," Joel said, as pleased to let us in on the information as we were to hear it.

It was a little amazing, really. Magiq had thrown his middle finger up at the industry from day one. His first track, "SAS," blazed. "SAS" was short for "Suits Ain't S**t." His lyrics came at you fast, like somebody pitching a dodgeball at your head. But if you kept up, you heard him airing all the ills of the music industry and clowning nearly every major label he could shout out. He wasn't just anti-mainstream, he was his own hate group. But a VGA would probably mean a label war—Magiq was gonna be paid in a few weeks. We knew it, so he had to.

"He wants a Flexx Unlimited makeover? How is that going to make up for him saying the only time he'd ever talk to a music executive was if they were in hell's waiting room together?" I asked, unconvinced that it would earn him forgiveness.

"He did go hard, didn't he?" Kara said, definite admiration in her voice.

"Hard is an understatement, honestly," I said, looking to Joel for answers.

He was smiling at us, enjoying the banter. For a second, I forgot we were lowly trainees.

"Well, our job isn't to get him a record deal." He stabbed his thick finger at the glossy photo. "His problem is, he has no look. Unless you consider looking like you've been sleeping under the overpass a look." He snorted. "Personally, I don't see one bit of a challenge in this. Anything we do is gonna be better than that." He glared at the photo disapprovingly. "But we get a lot of new clients from VGA word of mouth. So . . ."

"So, we get to make him over?" Kara said suspiciously.

I sat up, like a rod had snapped my back straight. "We finally get to style, like real style?" I asked, ideas bumping into each other inside my brain already.

"With my and Marques's guidance, yes," Joel confirmed. "I know I don't have to tell you what a big deal this is. Styling is usually reserved for senior staff. But Marshall and Manita—" He cleared his throat. "I mean, the Johnsons, are very interested in seeing how young people will style other young people. We'll check in with you daily on direction and concepts, but we're going to give you a lot of creative space."

Kara had scooted to the edge of her seat as Joel talked. "When do we get to meet Magiq?"

He frowned. "Rule number one, don't be starstruck. No asking for autographs. Or selfies." He laughed suddenly. "And please don't pull your phone out and ask him to say hey to your homegirl or whatever."

"Who is doing all that?" Kara asked, mouth scrunched in offense.

"We get plenty of interns who turn groupie once their favorite artist hit the style floor. Just saying, don't embarrass me," Joel said before turning the lecture directly to me. "All right now. I expect you to work together so Magiq has plenty of choices. This is a team project . . . at least for now."

"For now?" I asked.

He whizzed past my question, laying down the ground rules before shooing us away:

Work up concepts for approval;

Be inspired and use that inspiration;

Take it seriously;

Be ready for anything.

CHAPTER .18.

I was a mouse in the maze and the smell of cheese was strong.

I had so many ideas.

In the headshot Magiq was mean mugging. But there was something in his light brown eyes that didn't go with the head full of half loc'ed, mostly knotty hair. My fingers were itching to sketch out some ideas. I had to catch them while they were still pictures in my mind.

I grabbed my sketchbook and sat on the sofa in our style hub.

Kara put her hands on her hips. "What are you doing?"

I answered absently as I sketched. "I want to get a few ideas down."

"Joel said we have to talk it out first."

"I know. I'm—"

She sucked her teeth. "Look, if you gonna go ahead and do your own thing, fine. But I don't want hear nothing later when he ask if we followed directions."

My ideas were fading. Kara's insistence was like an alarm clock to a good dream.

"Now you care about following directions," I muttered.

"Yeah, I do," she snapped. "Joel said be inspired. I think we should look at catalogs to get ideas."

Joel said. Joel said. She hadn't cared what anybody said before and now it was Joel said. "Okay," I said reluctantly. "Just go grab some."

She scowled. "I'm your assistant now?"

"Kara, you the one who wants the catalogs." I sighed. "I wanted to draw some things first. Once I look at the catalogs, I'm gonna lose the ideas I have."

She turned heel and went to the circulation desk.

I went to scribble my idea, but it was gone.

Justice and Chandra came into the hub.

"This is going to be so much fun," Chandra said, before haul tailing it over to the circulation desk.

Justice sat on the round riser in front of the sofa. It was so low to the ground, his knees were almost the same height as his shoulders. I stared down at my sketch pad, willing the idea to reappear. When it didn't, I took a breath and said, "So y'all got STARZ, huh?"

He nodded.

"Let me guess, y'all gonna put them in miniskirts and crop tops," I said, trying to joke.

His lips disappeared for a second. "Even if we did, we gonna make it dope."

"I was just kidding," I said.

"If you say so," he said.

"Jus, why are you so mad?" I asked, my whine game strong.

His arms dangled from his knees. He looked at me like I'd asked him to pay me.

"No, I mean before Sammie went off on you," I said. My ears were on fire. Ms. Sadie said that meant somebody was talking about you. I scooted to the end of the sofa. Me and Justice were only about three inches apart. I talked above the activity around us. "What did I do? You haven't said boo to me since the program started."

"Mari, all I wanna do is get paid." He looked past me as he said, "Everything not about you."

I sat back, hard, against the sofa. "I never said it was."

"Then stop acting like it," he said.

He stood up as Chandra came back with her arms full of catalogs.

"Come on, Chandra. We can work at the desks," he said.

Kara came back, loaded down with thick, glossy catalogs. She spread them out on the table in front of the love seat, splaying them proudly. "If this not enough then we just not gonna find nothing." She plopped down opposite me on the love seat, legs crossed. Her right leg swung rhythmically as she thumbed through one of the catalogs full of the clothes we had access to. She looked up at me. "Did your idea ever come back?"

I shook my head. Words would mean tears. Either Kara didn't notice or didn't care.

She flipped through a few catalogs, making random suggestions. I didn't agree with any of them. Joel said we had to brainstorm. But in the end, she was going to do what she wanted and so was I.

I tuned her out, listening to Justice and Chandra talk about how to style the four girls who had won their high school talent show and were probably going to be the next big girls' group thanks to the VGA nod. Every now and then Chandra squealed. She did it every time she had a new idea. I bet the noise was driving Justice nuts. Whenever girls at school squealed he called it the White Girl Special.

He probably wished he could switch partners.

I did too.

Kara pulled me back.

"So, you have any thoughts on Magiq's new look?" She tugged at her hair, so it fell over her left shoulder. "Joel is right, though. Anything we come up with will be better than how he looks in that picture."

I doodled with my sketch maker app. Started drawing a male body.

"True," I said absently. I looked up and she was watching me. "I think better when I'm sketching."

She tried to peek at my sketch, so I turned it, showing it proud.

"You draw, huh?" She humphed under her breath. "I'm not artistic even a little bit."

"I thought you had to submit some kind of portfolio to get into the program?" I asked, my head back in the drawing.

"I didn't. Maybe everybody else did." I stared after her, confused, as she jumped up, swiped the folder with Magiq's photo in it from her desk, and sat back down. Started reading:

"Marvin Hakeem Sanders, born August fifth . . ." She

stopped abruptly. "Huh. His real name is Marvin." She scanned the page, reading a little to herself, then said, "How is some of this supposed to help us? Like his parents were middle-school teachers. And his father was shot when he was ten years old."

I explained how every client was interviewed and how the senior stylists used that information to help figure out what look the client could carry. She pushed back, but only a little bit.

"I don't know if I agree with all that," she said, going back to reading. "Hmm. So, his father, Sergio, had to stop teaching. He's sort of Magiq's manager." She looked up, nose wrinkled. "For real, I don't see how knowing that gonna help us."

"But it can though," I said. I tapped lightly, toggling from the Sketch app to my home screen. Sketch app. Home screen. Until they were a blur of color and graphics. "Does it say in there why he goes by the name Magiq?"

She flipped through the pages. I think she was ready to give up when she found it.

"Marvin chose the moniker Magiq as a nod to how much of what people really see about an artist is fake and sleight of hand. But he considers his lyrics real. 'They take away the smoke and mirrors,' Marvin says." She continued reading to herself, lips moving, and looked at me. "All right. But what does that mean? What does it have to do with what clothes we pick out for him?"

I tapped away, letting the idea form.

"For one of my ideas, I'm gonna hook him up with a military look," she said confidently. "He looks rough. I wanna put him in some camo and high black boots. His lyrics are so militant. The look would be dead-on him."

I totally disagreed. Military was too easy.

I reached for Magiq's glossy headshot and stared at it, letting it mix with the stuff Kara had read to me.

"Look at him," Kara said, pointing at his wild, knotted hair. "We keep his hair that way, add some of that black stuff athletes be wearing under their eyes. Make him look like he just stepped out of the jungle fighting."

"I know his lyrics are like eff the industry," I said.

She cocked her head at me. "Eff the industry. Really?" She shook her head, muttering to herself. She gave me the closest thing she'd ever given me to a smile as she mocked me. "Eff the industry." She snorted, then got serious again. "But go 'head."

I rolled my eyes, annoyed that she cut me off.

"Just saying that I agree his lyrics are harsh. But him looking homeless in this picture is still like . . ." I willed

Magiq's headshot to share its secret with me as I talked an idea out. "I think it's just him trying not to be what people expect. I think people would expect him to be militant."

"Exactly." Her eyebrows furrowed. "What's wrong with that? What are you gonna put him in?"

"His lyrics are pretty deep, right?" I asked.

She stared me in the face, intensely. I held her gaze, my face growing hot until she finally popped her eyebrow and said, "Yeah. Deep is one way of putting it."

"He be saying stuff like he knows what's up." I sat up straighter, feeling a style course through me. "Maybe he even knows somebody in the industry. Because he be calling them out about stuff that only somebody on the inside would know."

Kara scanned the notes. Her finger slid from left to right, quickly, then pointed. "Oh yup. His uncle was Rida T. Remember him?" She didn't wait for an answer. "Remember that song, 'Ride It, Get it'?" Her upper body bounced like she was in a car bumping on hydraulics as she sang, "Ride it, get it. Ride it, get it. Girls be on my tip because they ride it, get it."

"You are way too into that," I said, unable to stifle my laugh. "If Magiq needs a video chick, you got the job."

"Ha," she said real loud, then covered her mouth

when a few people looked over. She laugh-snorted. "No lie, I loved that song, though. My mother would turn it off when it played on the radio, because she said I had no idea what I was singing." Her head tilted in thought. "Wasn't that Rida T's only song?"

I sat up straight. "Wait. So, his uncle was a one-hit wonder. I bet Rida T dropped knowledge about the industry to him."

"Probably." She swished her hair to the right shoulder. "All right, so, great story. I'm sticking to my military look. What you come up with after all that?"

I tapped the picture as I stared at his face. What I had thought was that mean mugging was more like confidence. Like he knew something we didn't. "He's a music geek. I'm gonna play up his intellectual side."

"He doesn't look like he has an intellectual side." Kara snickered. She patted at her hair, thoughtfully. She kept the pat going, trying to soothe her freshly tightened bundles.

Just then Justice and Chandra walked over.

"Y'all got anything yet?" Chandra asked, clearly bubbling over with wanting to share hers.

"Yeah, so far, I'mma do a whole military camo look," Kara said. She nodded to me. "Mari gonna dress him like a basic White boy doing hip-hop."

My head popped up. She and Justice had a good time with that. Chandra snickered until she saw the look on my face.

"How is what I described a basic White boy?" I asked. "You act like Black people can't be geeks."

"You gonna dress him like a geek?" Justice asked, eyebrows furrowed. "Okay, then."

"Right? For real, the only thing Whiter is if he was dressed like he was ready go play golf," Kara said.

Chandra stood by helpless. Maybe she wanted to jump in, but she didn't.

Justice co-signing stung mad hard. At least he could have given me a chance to explain. I refused to let them see they were getting to me. I closed my sketch app and picked up Magiq's photograph again, pinching it hard so my fingers wouldn't tremble.

I put one hand over his body, so we only saw his face. His light brown eyes stared back at us defiantly. "Say what y'all want. Dude has intelligence in his eyes. And his lyrics are pretty deep for somebody only sixteen years old." Justice's arms were folded. Kara had her famous smirk on her face. I didn't back down. "Anytime somebody can talk for hours about something and break it down, no matter what that topic is . . . people usually call 'em a geek."

"All I know is, it's a lucky thing for you you can't be fired," Kara said. She stared in the direction of the circulation desk. "Anybody remember how we put in a request for inventory?"

"We had a whole orientation and you don't remember that?" Justice said, laughing, moving on without even commenting on what I'd said.

He and Kara walked off to the circulation desk together, with her admitting, "I'd be lying if I said I did."

For the second time that day, their laughter was a weight on my chest. I shrank away from the pity in Chandra's eyes and escaped into the comfort of my sketch app.

CHAPTER .19.

Like a human thermometer, Ms. Sadie noticed right away that something was different about me. She barely let me get in the house good before she declared, "Come and tell me how that job treating you."

I leaned into her, enjoying the hug of her tiny, strong arms.

"They're finally letting us style." I pecked her on the cheek, then slid into a chair at the table, my nose perking up. Garlic hummed through tendrils of steam floating above a bubbling pot of sauce. Mmm, rosé. Or "rosey," as Ms. Sadie called it.

I hadn't been hungry until I smelled it. I don't know how Ms. Sadie did it. She always made rosé when I needed my spirits lifted.

I took in the silent house marinating in the garlicky goodness. "Mommy and Daddy must not be here."

Bowls clanked as Ms. Sadie took them from the cupboard. "Well, they ain't. But what makes you say that?"

"You made my favorite," I said, scooting our bowls over to make way for the big platter of pasta she sat down.

She waved at the air. "That's only a coincidence. Keeping up with your parents' schedule is a fool's errand."

Didn't matter what she said, I had no doubt she knew exactly where my parents were. Ms. Sadie and coincidence didn't live in the same zip code. She knew things and when she didn't know, she wasn't afraid to ask loudly— like it irritated her to not know.

She muttered about busy schedules, then sat down waiting on me to bless the food. I did my usual prayer, thanking the Lord for the hands that prepared the food and praying for the safety of those missing from around the table. Ms. Sadie smiled, satisfied, and looked even more pleased when I piled my bowl high.

The rosé was a nice change from her fried and salty dinners and she only ever served it when me and her were solo because Daddy said the cream sauce was too rich and Mommy didn't do carbs. It was our meal. I speared a few pieces of pasta, loving how the sauce clung to it.

Ms. Sadie took a delicate bite, then placed her fork down like she was full. She put her chin in her hand. "That job agreeing with you?" Her eyebrow rose.

"It's okay. I'm glad we finally doing real work."

She didn't bother pretending she wanted to hear about that. "Umhm. So, the other kids real nice?"

I don't know why adults ask that question. There's no right answer. Not once have I ever gotten along with every person I met. Rather than admit that Justice wasn't talking to me and Kara basically hated me, I focused on Chandra. Before I knew it, I had her cackling about Chandra's motor mouth. But she wouldn't be Ms. Sadie if she hadn't chirped, "Umhm. Now what you think they all saying 'bout you?"

I shrugged. "What don't they already know about me?"

"Reading about you in a magazine not the same as knowing you." Her fork tinged as she tapped it on her bowl. "What they saying 'bout you? Now that they with you?"

"Who knows," I said, my throat dry.

Which wasn't a lie. I didn't know. Not really.

"Your little friend Justin doing good too?"

Her eyes crinkled in the corners, like she was holding back a smile.

"Justice, Ms. Sadie. And he's fine," I said, stuffing a forkful of pasta into my mouth so I didn't do something stupid like ask Ms. Sadie, of all people, for advice on a boy.

"Just fine?" That eyebrow went high again. "Much as y'all two talk. He just fine?"

Her voice went high, in a bad imitation of me. Her tiny shoulders shook as she laughed at my eye roll.

"We don't get to talk a lot," I said. "But he doing all right . . . from what I can tell."

She speared a piece of pasta, talking more to it than me. "Hmmph, I thought y'all be together all day, every day. That ain't the case?" She popped it into her mouth and studied me as she chewed.

I let more truth slide out. "No, we are. But I think he like one of the other girls, so . . ." I shrugged.

"Well if he do, he do. He can be friends with more than one person at a time," Ms. Sadie said.

"He sure can," I said, swallowing against the lump in my throat. Not like Ms. Sadie would understand how complicated it was. How different Justice was being. How unwelcome I felt when I was around him.

"Maybe he was only tight with me because he wanted to get a job at Flexx," I said, the words out before I could stop them.

"Do you believe that?" Annoyed by my constant shrugging, she gave me one of those you-got-one-more-time looks as she went on. "It's always gonna be people who want something from you. Up to you whether you let 'em use you or not. Seems to me y'all two were friends way before this new program came to be."

Little firecrackers went off in my heart. I latched on. If Ms. Sadie thought Justice was real, that was enough for me.

"You right. I think he likes Kara though."

"You said that already."

I kept my annoyance in check. "Girlfriend like, Ms. Sadie."

Her bushy brows furrowed. "Kara. That another little girl in the program?"

I nodded, then beat her to the punch. "Her last name is Knight." I laughed. "But, no, I don't know her mother."

I figured she would laugh with me. If you were Black and from District City, Ms. Sadie was always gonna ask two questions—What's their last name? and Who's their momma? Instead, she pressed her fat knuckles down on the table to help push herself up out of the chair. She took her plate and shuffled over to the sink, doing that magic trick of aging in front of my eyes.

I talked over the running water. "Then again, she from Holly Heights. Jus is a private school dude now. Probably too soft for her."

Ms. Sadie whipped around, arms folded. "You know better than that. Don't go talking that nonsense, putting people in boxes 'cause of where they from. That little girl ain't no different than you or nobody else out here trying find a way for herself."

My eyebrows dipped in confusion. "I was just joking."

"It's not funny, Marigold. And if you acting like you better than people, then I got an idea what them other kids think about you."

That stung. When was anybody going to care about how they acted made me feel?

I rose up, defending myself.

"I wasn't acting like—"

"You better not be," she snapped, then turned her attention back to the sink.

I snatched my bowl off the table and dumped the rest of the pasta into the trash can.

"How come it's okay for everybody to judge me? But the second I say something I'm the one wrong?" I stomped as hard as I dared from the trash can to the sink, where I stood inches behind her, my bowl extended so she could take it. I pouted as I ranted. "When I'm being called snobby or being teased 'cause my parents have money, it's all good. All I said was she from Holly. And she is. She Holly all day and proud."

Ms. Sadie's shoulders sagged and I heard her sigh as she stopped tumbling the dishes in the water. She wiped her hands and faced me. "What other choice she have but to be proud, Marigold? She can't help where she from." She plucked the bowl from my hands and let it sink into the soapy water. "You think she like being from a neighborhood most known for how poor everyone is?"

"I didn't say all that, Ms. Sadie," I said, the fight already fizzling out of me.

She took my hands into her soft damp ones and squeezed.

"If the worst thing that's happening to you is people teasing you for having food on the table and a roof over your head, then you still having a better day than most. Hear?" Her eyebrow pitched again. "Hear?"

"Yes ma'am," I said quietly.

Her grip eased. Her sharp words didn't. "Ain't nothing uglier than when girls fight."

"Fight? Ms. Sadie, nobody gonna fight," I said, keeping my eye roll in check.

She looked at me in each eyeball, like she was going to find some new truth in one of them. "I know you know better. I can't speak for the other little girl. But sometimes things run deeper than you understand, with people. Focus on the work. You and that little boy still be friends when this all over and y'all back at school."

With that she went back to the dishes, dismissing me.

CHAT-TER

Cha-Cha:

Bruh we're really for really real
styling a celebrity 🤩 🖤 🖤

Mari_Golden:

did M&J approve your outfit yet?

Cha-Cha:

Not yet. Said I need to work on
making it a full look . . . what do
you think?

She sent me a photo of two outfits on mannequins.
One had on a sparkly red halter top and hot pants to
match, the other a red minidress with sequins.

Mari_Golden:

It's cute. The red sparkles match, but
tbh they're still two different looks. You
know? And STARZ is a group so. . .

Cha-Cha:

maybe stick with the halter and
hot pants OR the minidress?

Mari_Golden:

I don't wanna tell u how to do it. It
looks cool but yeah it's not a full look.

Cha-Cha:

For real I want your advice.

#NoHurtFeelings

Mari_Golden:

please don't take it personal. I'm
serious.

Cha-Cha:

✌️ promise

Mari_Golden:

what about instead of halter and
hot pants, a body suit but with like a
mini-skirtlet attached. Keep the mini
dress. BUT make 'em both leather or
something instead of sparkles. Sorry.
just not a big fan of the sparkly stuff.

Cha-Cha:

. . .

Mari_Golden:

Or stay w/what you got. For real. I'm
just talking. ☺

Cha-Cha:

Um no you're right! Cause the
skirtlet and the mini dress are
sort of like different ways to do a

"dress." I like that. Okay I'm gonna

look for that in the catalog.

Mari_Golden:

You don't have to take the idea.

Seriously, Chandra.

Cha-Cha:

I love it. I'm not just saying that. I

appreciate u being honest w/me.

Mari_Golden:

Okay, cool. I just don't want you to feel

like you gotta always be nice to me.

I promise I'm not running and telling

everything that happens.

Cha-Cha:

who thinks that?

Mari_Golden:

🪦 just setting record straight

Cha-Cha:

We good. I'm glad me and you not

competing against each other.

Mari_Golden:

Thanks? 🫤

Cha-Cha:

LOL yes, thanks cause if we were

you wouldn't have helped me.

Mari_Golden:
big facts 😂

Cha-Cha:
This time next week one or both
of us gonna have our outfit on the
VGA red carpet 😱 I'm sure it ain't
no big deal to you though. But I
can barely sleep at night I'm so
daggone wired.

Mari_Golden:
Don't get it twisted, I'm excited too. I
hope Magiq picks mine. I don't mean
any harm but Kara's military look isn't
all that original.

Cha-Cha:
TBH it doesn't really make him
over. He kinda already look like
that.

Mari_Golden:
IKR. But #NoScreenShots

Cha-Cha:
nevah that. I got you, Sis

It was too late to take back what I'd texted. Chandra

could drop what I'd said in their group text—turn both Justice and Kara against me.

Ahh look, Mari talking mess, y'all.

Waves of regret washed gently over me as I wondered why I'd been that honest?

I knew why, though.

I wanted to believe Chandra had my back. Believe that somebody liked having me in the program. Believe that giving her advice (that she asked for) helped me fit in. Finally.

CHAPTER .20.

The year I turned nine was the year everyone at school suddenly got curious about my family's business. What exactly was a hip-hop media company? What does it do? How does it work?

Being Black must be so fascinating. Please, Marigold, teach us your ways.

Mommy said it's because every kid, at some point, is gonna talk out of turn and reveal where their parents' hearts really lie.

Daddy said that was the year people finally put their hoods on. I didn't get it, at first. Didn't understand that he was talking about Klan hoods and saying that all the people who automatically assumed he'd started Flexx from money he'd made selling drugs were being racist. By the middle of the school year, the list of people wearing their hoods was way longer than the list of people I still hung out with.

The first person to dig was Lana. I remember how cold and blue her pool water was that day. How the orange and yellow inflatable boat we'd been pushing each other in, floated gently by itself like a ghost had taken over as captain. How one minute we were sitting on the side of the pool, giggling, kicking our feet to see if the ripples we made would make the boat come toward us or away, and the next minute she was sitting cross-legged, leaning over, whispering curiously, "Have you ever gone on a drug deal with your dad?"

It was the way she assumed it was true that hurt. It was my gut telling me that she would have never asked any of our White friends that question that made it easy to always be busy every time she asked me about coming over after that. It didn't take her long to get bored of chasing after me before she moved on. I don't think we've said fifty words to each other since.

Maybe it sounds stupid, but I had never felt how Black I was until that year. That was when Mommy helped Flo-A form the I & D Committee and got rid of dress code rules like no braids or locs. It got easier to avoid anybody who was I'm-not-racist-but-why-do-we-need-Black-History-Month? fake woke.

Then, the very next summer, Sammie's friends stripped me of my Black card by making everything a joke.

How I talked.

How I dressed.

How I wore my hair.

Or they'd make up wild rumors about life in T-Hill that didn't make any sense. Are gold toilets even a thing?

The difference was, I never told Mommy or Daddy about it. It wasn't like Sammie's clique was being racist, even if they did make me feel just as empty and hurt as the jokes from White people. I stuck it out, pretending to be okay with them "playing around," happy when Sammie finally defended me and told her friends going in on me was played out.

It never stopped stinging that there wasn't anything I could do to be Black enough.

Style High wasn't exactly like that summer, but close. The way Justice was—like everything I said was low-key annoying or embarrassing him—I obviously wasn't Black enough for him and I was tired of trying to prove it. How do you even prove Blackness?

I threw myself into selecting every piece, every accessory I could find for Magiq's outfits, talking them over in mandatory meetings with Joel every afternoon. They made each of us come up with three different ways to show off our style idea. I soaked in every chance they gave us to work on finding pieces.

We still spent the mornings doing our usual chores, since thanks to the VGAs there was even more demand for inventory to be in the right place. The first day, I spoke up and said I was going to be the runner. Justice looked surprised that I wasn't letting him supervise anymore. But he didn't reject me. It was nice walking through the building alone, lost in the music streaming through my buds. I took my time, making sure to get all the pickups done. It was so much better than being in the storeroom not knowing what to say to Kara that wouldn't end in an annoyed eye roll. Even though Chandra mostly co-signed any conversation I started, the tension was real.

The third day in a row, I did it again, calling the job as we walked to the storeroom.

Kara challenged Justice. "We picking our own jobs now?"

I was grateful when Chandra said, "I'm good with that. I'll do shoes and accessories today."

"Not it on steamer," Kara said quickly, when she saw she either had to pick a job or be stuck with one.

"It don't matter," Justice said, turning the steamer on.

"Not now that you don't have a choice," I said. I had meant it as a joke but kind of liked that Kara snickered. I could roll off mean jokes, too.

It was a small win. But I took it.

I didn't have time to savor it. Marques walked into the storeroom, looking around curiously. No doubt to make sure we understood he didn't grace this part of the building with his presence very often.

He waited until all our attention was on him.

"I'm pleased to inform you that Joel and I have accepted your concepts for your clients." He bowed his head, so we obliged with a tiny smattering of applause.

I looked at Justice, to share a smile at how silly it felt to clap, but he was engrossed—steamer hissing forgotten in his hand.

Marques tucked an invisible stray hair behind his ear. As if he'd ever have a hair out of place. He plucked colored index cards from the notebook he was holding, handing each of us one.

"Head to the style hub listed on your card. There are models waiting for you."

"Models," Chandra squealed with a clap.

"That's what's up," Justice said, pumping the steamer hose in victory.

Even Kara looked mildly impressed, eyebrow cocked in curiosity.

I shifted from one foot to the other, ready to play dress-up.

Marques put his hand up, silencing any further murmuring. "You'll have forty-five minutes to style your models, then send them to the orange hub." His small shoulders hitched up then down as he exhaled dramatically. "Okay, well . . . let's see what y'all got."

He walked away, then stopped when he realized we weren't behind him.

"Today," he commanded with a shake of his head. "Your time starts the second you reach the Closet."

That got us moving. My short legs carried me past everyone. My fingers itched to turn all the photos and swatches I'd picked out into real fashion. Chandra bubbled excitedly in the elevator. When the doors opened on the Closet's floor, we dashed out like reality TV stars under a time challenge.

I took a second to enjoy being in a style hub, alone, with three models dressed in tee shirts and jeans, waiting for me to make them over. Me.

The music felt extra loud today, like the whole room was celebrating our arrival.

That was my imagination, for sure. But it felt good.

I ran my fingers over the neat stacks of clothes representing what I'd picked out of inventory and got to work. In my head, I named the models, Whisper Wayne, Jumpy Jarrett, and Total Model Guy, who was killing it by doing everything I asked like I was the one paying him. He was my favorite, so I ended up switching outfits between him and Jumpy so that TMG had on the outfit I hoped Magiq would pick.

When Joel walked up next to me, I had finished with five minutes to spare and was talking to Whisper—my neck stretched so I could catch what he was saying. Like, dude, speak up.

"Do you need them to model for you?" I asked, assuming Joel was here to pick the winning outfit to present to Magiq.

Joel gave them a quick glance. "Nope. You can lead them down to the orange hub."

I frowned. "All of 'em?"

"Yes, ma'am," Joel said as he gave my shoulder a double tap. "Time's up."

"How do they look?" I asked, eager for feedback.

"Dressed," he said, then laughed. "At this point, what I say doesn't matter."

"Not even a little thumbs-up or down, Jay? Please."

He laughed, walked ahead of me, and joined Marques in the trainees' hub.

It was set up like we were ready to play a round of Family Feud.

I joined Chandra on the orange loveseat. Kara and Justice sat on a purple loveseat across from us. I shut up the voice in my head nudging me to analyze how close she sat to Justice. Refusing to think about how fast he'd traded in our friendship for a lil' summer crush.

The round risers for our mannies had been replaced with a runway going from the back of the hub to the front.

Marques and Joel stood on it, both at home as the center of attention.

"All right, kiddies, listen up," Marques said, even though we were focused on them already. We knew when it was showtime. "I'm not gonna lie. You all have worked hard. Snap for that." He snapped once in the air, seemingly unbothered that we didn't snap back.

The dueling love seats meant we were about to critique each other. The challenge was thick in the air. This was it. We were going to have to be real.

I yawned to release some of the tension in my face.

Joel, the mother hen, clucked at me. "Party too hard this weekend, Ms. Johnson?"

I eked out a smile and shook my head.

"I should hope not. Until the VGAs are over, this project should be all anybody is thinking about." He gave everyone a quick evil eye for good measure.

Kara sat up straighter like she was ready to spring.

"You've picked out your looks and your client has given preliminary approval," Marques said.

Joel continued, their routine well-oiled by now.

"Now your fellow stylists will have a chance to comment and suggest enhancements."

Our collective groan wasn't lost in the Closet's usual chatter.

Enhancements?

"Aww man," Justice muttered.

"But what if the client doesn't like the changes?" Kara asked, looking over at me and Chandra like one of us had suddenly farted.

"And do we get to veto it if we don't like their 'enhancements,'" asked Chandra, puffed up beside me. She threw herself back on the sofa, arms folded.

Justice smoothed his eyebrows. "Do we at least get to

explain the inspiration for our style? 'Cause they might change something that we did on purpose," he said.

I hated it, like everybody else. I also knew grumbling wasn't gonna cut it.

"We warned you about this. I'm not sure why everyone is up in arms," Marques said, sounding like he'd been schooling us for months instead of just weeks.

"Look, y'all." Joel walked to the middle of the runway. "Nobody likes having their styles ripped apart. But there's a reason we work in teams around here. Sometimes someone catches what you didn't. How come you're all assuming that the feedback is going to be negative?"

He actually waited for an answer.

What were we going to say?

That it was real now and it was about more than picking apart outfits.

I didn't want anybody telling me what I left out or could do better. Even if their suggestion did make it better. Especially if their suggestion made it better.

I was going to say that?

Nope. I clammed up like everybody else.

Joel took a deep breath and shook his head.

"Y'all are still in this together, you know? I mean you styled your own look, but . . . you're still one team."

Marques seemed better at reading the mood. He stepped forward on the slim runway, forcing Joel to take a step back.

"This is a competitive industry. It's smart of you to watch your own backs." He studied us, then he put his teacher's voice back on. "Justice, if you need to explain to make people understand your fashion choices then your team is in trouble. And I'm not even kidding. If people don't 'get' your fashion choices, then chances are you went wrong somewhere." He clapped his hands. "Enough. Models for Team STARZ, come!"

I blew a big sigh of relief that I wasn't up first and felt Chandra shift away from me. I gave her an apologetic leg pat.

"Based on what you showed me, last, I'm sure you killed it," I whispered.

"I thought so," she said, a little snip in her voice.

Marques and Joel stepped off the runway and four girls came from the dressing room. Two in Chandra's look, two in Justice's. She'd taken my advice and went with the leather look. It was even better than I had envisioned.

In pairs, the models took a turn coming down the runway, then they fanned out, so we could study them.

"Thoughts?" Marques asked from behind us.

"I really like models three and four," I said.

Beside me, Chandra vibrated happily. Her leg touched mine as she leaned closer.

Kara immediately jumped on Justice's bandwagon. "I like one and two better. The frilly skirt paired with the combat boots is hot."

I treaded carefully. "I didn't say I didn't like them. Except maybe go a little easy on the makeup."

"See, that's what I mean," said Justice. He cut his eyes at me. "I picked that style for Jamay. Her profile request said she into making her eyes dramatic." He put his hands up like, I give up. "That's why I asked could we at least explain."

"Yeah, but just 'cause she like dramatic makeup don't mean you automatically go with it," Chandra argued. She turned and threw it on Marques's lap. "Didn't you tell us that sometimes you gotta give the client what's right even if it's not what they like?"

Marques chest puffed with pride as he nodded in agreement.

"It's not that the outfit doesn't work," I said, trying my best to make up. "But the eyeliner is kind of heavy."

Justice rolled his eyes at me.

"Youno the whole story," he said. He wriggled up

until he was near the edge of the love seat, his legs like two long toothpicks jutting from the small seat. "I was trying to compromise. I kept some things Jamay was feeling, like the big hoop earrings. But I purposely did the lacy-looking skirt because normally she's straight tomboy."

"The outfit looks fine," I pleaded. "Is it really a big deal if you have to tone down her eye makeup?"

"Not a big deal to you," he said.

The models stood, faces neutral, accepting our critique without emotion. "All good, respectful feedback," Joel said.

"Take notes, STARZ team," Marques said, prompting us to continue commenting. Kara only said enough to keep Marques and Joel from calling her out for not being honest, basically letting me and Chandra drag Justice by ourselves. She sat back, her face half hidden by Justice's shoulder. I raised my eyebrow at her and she shrugged.

Justice sat stony faced.

I cleared my throat.

"I like the skirt and the top." I paused, wanting to stop there. Marques and Joel seemed to expect more. I quickly added, letting the words run together. "Idon'treallylovetheboots."

"I already said I like the look. The boots, too," Kara

said, immediately winning a point from Justice, judging by the look of smug satisfaction on his face.

Then even Chandra waffled. "The boots fine with me."

Justice took notes, jaw tight.

Joel dismissed the models with a polite "Thank you, ladies," then called out, "Let me get my Magiq clones out here."

Kara scooted to the edge of the love seat, her face glowing. I shrank back, afraid of what was coming until I saw Kara's military look next to my bookworm with swag vibe.

I still adored my idea. Total Model Guy flossed perfectly.

I loved the ankle-length black-and-gray-plaid skinny-suit pants and how they weren't sure if they were business or casual. I paired them with a gray twill blazer with a single button that I'd kept undone, and a nice pressed black T-shirt and blindingly white tennas. No socks, of course. It was all topped off with a gray golf cap and a pair of black square-framed glasses.

Justice came out of the gate. "Not trying to be ignorant, but all that gray is boring. He going to an award show, not to teach a college class."

"I wouldn't say it was boring," Chandra said, glancing my way.

"Whatever, Jus. It's clean and since Magiq don't take a lot of photos nobody knows what his style is. It's not my fault that I did something besides the obvious," I said.

"Oh, so me and Kara's stuff was obvious, now?" he growled.

"Let's not attack," Joel said. He stepped in between the two love seats, wide body blocking us from catting at each other.

Justice's voice rose above the Closet's growing noise. "It's not even that serious. Just 'cause you went all CSI and dug into my man's whole entire life to come up with a style, don't mean yours better, Marigold."

I leaned so I could see around Joel, refusing to give in. "I didn't even say mine was better. I said mine not as obvious."

"But you think it's better. Everybody know that's what you mean."

"Everybody who?" My voice was high-pitched and indignant. I raised a brow at Chandra. "You think that?"

Her mouth dropped open and she looked to Joel for help.

"That's enough, you two," Marques said.

"Everybody mean everybody," Justice said with force.

Marques raised his voice. "I mean it. That's enough. We

asked for your opinion and you gave it. If you're this mad about what your friends saying, what are you going to do when your clients tell you they don't like something?"

He looked from me to Justice, Chandra to Kara.

Our faces were long. We'd all just been to the same funeral.

The one that rest in peaced me and Justice's friendship.

CHAPTER .21.

Got_Sammit:

You just hurt his feelings. He be

alright.

Mari_Golden:

I don't care if he is.

Got_Sammit:

You do though. 😆

Mari_Golden:

Nope. I don't. I been worried about
his feelings. Kara's feelings. Chandra's
feelings this whole time. Nobody cares
about mine. It's dead.

Got_Sammit:

Umph. You know I got you,

however you wanna roll. 👊

Mari_Golden:

Thanks, Sis. 🖤

I sat in my window seat, knees to my chest, staring down at Sammie's messages. I never heard Daddy come in until his large frame squeezed into the space left on the seat. His voice startled me.

"Good gossip or wild video?"

"Daddy. Hey." I opened my arms, squeezing hard when he leaned in. I swallowed the tears clogging my throat. "Neither. Chatting with Sammie. How was your trip?"

"Over. Glad to be home with my girls." He was dressed in his flying clothes—black T-shirt, black track pants with a white stripe down the side, and black sneakers. It made him look like he'd just freshened up after a pickup basketball game. He stretched out his long legs. "How you liking y'all special project? Did your pops hook y'all up or what?" He put his hand out for a high five and I tapped it as he kept congratulating himself. "Got y'all working on the VGAs. Y'all better do right by Flexx. This as big a deal as you can get."

"Believe me, I think everybody might be willing to

work for you for free, after this." I added, "Except me. Style High cool. But pass me my cash."

He tweaked my toe. "Talk to my banker. She downstairs."

"It's been okay. I mean I love styling. It got a little ugly today." I hugged my knees. Daddy listened quietly, letting me tell the story. He laughed when I imitated Marques or Joel. Anger burned as I told him about Justice ripping my outfit.

"Him and Kara probably side chatting now talking smack about me," I said, with a shrug I didn't mean. I was mad at Justice. I didn't even care that he was mad, too. I cared that he had somebody on his side, probably blowing his head up instigating.

"Until today, were you and Kara getting along?" he asked.

I scowled. "Not really."

He bit his lip, opened his mouth to say something and I interrupted. "I'm not tripping over that though. Everybody not meant to be friends." I tapped at my phone, watching the backlight glow. "I didn't think Justice would take what I said like that. But him and Kara caping so hard for each other. It's annoying."

Daddy crossed his arms. "If Yes Sir's feelings too soft then maybe he not cut out for fashion or basketball." I knew he was teasing, but I wasn't in the mood to joke. He leaned back, settling in for a story when a message rang in. I brought the phone to my face, greedily lapping up the message.

Cha-Cha:

I know this is foul but . . . I

thought you would want to know

I squinted at the screenshot, my stomach curling into itself as I absorbed the words.

KarasDa1:

She def carried you today.

JayRocks:

If it was just us it wouldn't matter.

who knows what M&J go back and

tell the Johnsons

Cha-Cha:

okay but when we not honest

M&J make us talk. She just did it

before they forced it, for real

KarasDa1:

there you go up her butt. Even if they

keep pushing you can find ways. I didn't

say that much and they ain't call me

out.

JayRocks:

facts

KarasDa1:

And y'all supposed to be tight. It was
like she did it on purpose trying show
everybody up

JayRocks:

😕

KarasDa1:

 Of course M&J ended up liking her
outfit more than mine. Like whet? 😑
Gon' have Magiq out here looking like a
whole golf caddy

JayRocks:

😂😂😂 not the golf caddy. It's
not a lie, tho.

Daddy's voice called me back. "And in conclusion, you have to be able to take criticism in this business. Thanks for coming to my TED talk even though you didn't hear nothing I said once that phone went off."

I turned the phone on its face and sat it near my butt. I talked through my pounding chest, wanting to be alone so I could read the message again. "Sorry. You right, though. Jus will get over it . . . probably."

"No probably in it," Daddy said. He stood up. "All of you gotta move on. It's the clients' turn to weigh in on Monday."

"True." My phone dinged again. I kept my face up to my father.

"And don't be too hard on Kara or Chandra either. I'm sure the scrutiny Marques put on you all is enough to make anybody tread lightly."

"Hmmph, nah."

He looked at me quizzically. "Nah what?"

"Chandra maybe. Kara say whatever she want any other time. She just didn't want Justice to be mad at her."

A flurry of messages came in. I pushed the warm phone away, keeping my hand on top so I could flip it as soon as Daddy left.

"Should I say something to Marques and Joel? Maybe have them step in to help y'all get along?" His voice was uncertain, like when he'd normally turn to Mommy and let her decide. I wanted to get to my phone too bad for conversation or another one of his stories. I said, "Umem, it's whatever," and gave myself credit for not looking down at the phone as another message chimed in. Since my father seemed like he needed more, I said, "I don't need any more smoke, Daddy. You know if Marques and Joel say something then everybody gonna swear I ran crying to you."

His eyes crinkled in concern. I felt a hardcore lesson coming.

I stood up, stretching. "I'm not gonna lie, I thought it was going to be different between me and Justice." I muttered the truth, "Maybe I shouldn't have ever done the program." He touched my shoulder and my eyes itched with tears.

"Try to understand that he's approaching Style High with a different energy than you. He can't help it no more than you can help the way you come at it." His hand squeezed lightly. "But that doesn't mean you have to ever hide your talent or fake a comment. It'll be all good on Monday. Watch."

I nodded.

He kissed my forehead. "Go on and check your phone. I see you, feigning. G'night. Love you."

"Love you too. Night, Daddy," I said, scrolling before he was out the door.

CHAPTER .22.

I spent the entire weekend one Send away from forwarding Justice the screenshots. I only didn't because Chandra immediately had regrets and blew up my phone begging me not to let them know she'd snitched.

I didn't care about them being mad with her. I really didn't. But she could have kept the screenshots to herself. And she didn't. I owed her.

I wrote then deleted ten different messages to Sammie, daydreaming about her rolling up on Justice and getting dead into his stuff. I didn't do that, either.

We only had one more week of Style High. If he wanted to spend it mad, so could I. And the sooner I got away from Kara, the better. I'd spend the rest of the summer tagging behind Ms. Sadie at Beth U moping until Sammie got off work. Hard to believe, I was looking forward to it.

On Sunday, I planned how I was going to act like nothing was wrong on Monday.

Well, nothing was wrong with me. So, it would be easy to do. Then I saw a picture on Justice's Buzz TL, him, Kara, and some girl I didn't know. They were at the zoo, him sandwiched between them. Kara's round face looking gleeful, cheeks plump, teeth shining enough for me to count both rows. The other girl giving face with a head tilt angled so deep it rested on Justice's shoulder. Hashtags for days.

#DatCrew
#ZooCrew
#HotAsHale
#DeyGonTrip
#Saturday
#ScurredofLions
#IfIRunYouBetterRunWitMe

I messaged Justice, tears blurring the letters, not bothering to correct typos.

That's so mesed up abut you

JayRocks:

what I do now?

Mari_Golden:

are you seriusly mad? Crits are part of teh program. What I said wasn't personal.

JayRocks:

imma keep it a stack. You came off like I ain't know what I was doing. I don't need Marques going back and telling your Pops my skills lacking

Mari_Golden:

they 👏 asked 👏 us 👏 for 👏 feedback. Everybody got it! Not just you.

JayRocks:

you always try make it like it's not a big deal just cause it's not for you.

Mari_Golden:

I want to do good like everybody else 🙈

JayRocks:

But u don't HAVE to do good.

Mari_Golden:

Wowww.

JayRocks:

You don't though.

Mari_Golden:

I don't have no pressure on me to do
good, Justice? None? Wow. Ok

JayRocks:

you working real hard to be
oppressed, rn

Mari_Golden:

and you real wild, right now! Are u mad
w/Kara like u mad w/me?

JayRocks:

you need ease up off her. I don't
think you want be on her bad side.

Mari_Golden:

what does that mean? 🫣

JayRocks:

Nothing. You brought her up.
What she gotta do with this?

Mari_Golden:

She ain't say much but she did say
something. But you didn't seem mad
w/her. #ZooCrew 🙄

JayRocks:

oh you stalking like a mug. And
she didn't go in on my model.

Mari_Golden:

W/E b/c she played dumb I HAD to say
stuff

JayRocks:

ain't nobody make you

Mari_Golden:

If you like Kara just say so. She probably
just playing you anyway.

JayRocks:

👌

Mari_Golden:

Same! ✌️

CHAPTER .23.

"**P**retty girls like pretty boys. And pretty boys like pretty toys," Kara sang, the melody just reaching my ears through the noise of the Closet.

It was mad busy. Every single style hub was a flurry of hands primping, patting, and pulling at clothes to make them hang right; models patiently being fussed over; publicists on phones with their heads bent away from the noise, like there was actually a spot that was quiet.

I inhaled the energy and worked in my bubble. Letting Kara work in hers.

By the time Magiq eased his way into our hub, looking like he wanted to be anywhere else but there with two newbie stylists trying not to step on each other's toes as we laid out his VGA outfits, I was too caught up in wanting him to like my work to worry about Justice or Kara.

Magiq's publicist, a Latina chick with lips and a butt that looked like someone had inflated her with Botox, and his Dadager finally left him to us, disappearing back into the elevator after confirming we only had an hour. Either they trusted us or figured we'd be easy to overrule.

Magiq stood at the edge of the hub. I almost expected him to clutch his drabby army fatigue jacket close to him, daring us to take it off.

Kara approached him first. "It's good to meet you. I'm Kara."

My eyes almost popped out of my head. So, she had manners when she wanted to.

She turned her head to me, my cue. I put my hand out for a shake, determined to be even more professional than her. "I'm Marigold Johnson. Nice to meet you."

He shook my hand. I tried to continue talking but Kara jumped back in, making me look like her assistant.

"Look, if you don't like what we picked out, just say so," she said, gesturing to the two mannies outfitted in our selections. "You gotta be coolin' for real at the VGAs. So, don't go along with nothing if you think the outfit janked."

I inhaled, ready to blurt, Hold up, when Magiq cracked the closest thing to a smile I'd ever seen on any pictures of him.

He plucked at his jacket.

"I'm fine wearing this then, right?"

Kara laughed, instinctively knowing it was a joke. I forced a titter, praying Magiq didn't call her bluff. Kara, her round face smiling up at Magiq said, "We hooked you up, big. You gonna like it."

I took a step forward, so me and Kara were side by side. "We hoping you'll work with us though. It would make Flexx look bad if we didn't put our own touch on it a little. It's the VGAs, right? Represent."

Magiq put his fist out for a tap. He looked from one mannie to the other.

"True. True." He pulled at some barely-there hair on his chin. "I mean, for real, what y'all picked wasn't bad. Both looks dope."

Kara grinned big, the only sign that she'd been as worried about Magiq's response as I'd been. She knew he had to pick one of our outfits. There were no backups. Kara explained that even though the mannies were dressed in what we'd styled, we had duplicates laid out in the dressing room already.

Magiq walked around the mannies, looking them up and down, checking out every piece of clothing.

"And don't laugh," Kara said, as gentle as I'd ever heard her. "But I was thinking you could wear like that black stuff under your eyes if you pick the military one. Your lyrics be so hardcore it seem like you going to war with somebody."

"That's word," he said.

She cheesed back at him.

I pointed to my outfit hanging on the manny. "What do you think?"

"I'm a geek, huh?" Magiq asked. The intelligence I'd seen flashed bright. His eyes shifted from left to right. "The secret's out. Just keep that on the low, though."

I crossed my heart. "Client/stylist privilege."

Kara's eyes flitted nervously from me to the way Magiq rubbed the material of the pants between his fingers, testing how it felt. I pressed on, smelling a victory. Wanting it.

"You be dropping mad knowledge in your lyrics. I can tell you know stuff everybody doesn't. It's like an inside joke or something."

"Mos def," Magiq said.

Kara put her hand on her mannie's shoulder. "Let us

know which one you feeling the most. I show you to the dressing room."

"I'mma try on both," he said. "Only thing about that one—" He nodded to mine. "I don't know about the skinny pants. They a little . . ."

"Too tight," Kara said, phony sweet.

He chuckled. "A lil' bit."

I tugged at the pants near the thigh. "Nope. They have a little bit of spandex in 'em. Not tight at all."

"Oh, all right. That's what's up," he said, nodding.

When he came out in Kara's outfit, she worked the room. Talking his ear off about going to battle and going to war. Just a few days ago, she didn't understand why an outfit needed a story. Today, she couldn't shut up.

I stood nearby, watching her adjust the pants legs— so tight at the bottom he probably was going to need help getting them off—and stuttering through her answer when Magiq pointed out how hot the jacket was and how if he took it off the whole thing didn't work the same.

Ha. Exactly.

When it was my turn, she sat on the love seat giving me more space than I had given her. Oh well. I didn't fuss over Magiq. He stood in front of the mirrors, turning to see every angle. I made sure to talk loud, so she could hear me. "The jacket is real light. I don't think you'll need to take it off."

"That's what's up," he said.

I didn't care that he sounded like a parrot that only knew three words.

He liked my outfit. I felt it.

He buttoned and unbuttoned the blazer. Did that thing people do when they're feeling good about what they're wearing. He put one foot out, leaned back and pretended to pose for a camera. I pretended to snap a pic. I knew Kara was behind me, burning hot. So I turned it up a notch.

"Hold up." I ran and got my phone, took a real photo. Handed him my phone. "Send it to yourself."

He did before returning to the dressing room.

Kara was by my side like she had wheels.

"You can't do that," she whispered angrily.

"Do what?" I asked, saving the pic.

"He has to decide, now. You think you slick letting him take a picture so he have your outfit memorized."

I'd had enough. I crossed my arms. "Don't be mad at me because you didn't think to take a picture."

Her mouth hung open. She fiddled with her weave, a

mass of curls that made her look like a poodle. I could see her wanting to ask Magiq if he'd put her outfit back on again so she could flick it up. But he was out, in his old drabby clothes before she had a chance.

"Ay, so both outfits was fire. No lies," he said. Kara looked hopeful for a second, but the lights in her eyes went out as he said, "I'mma kick it with the suit pants. I'm digging that one a little bit more."

I could have been petty and celebrated. Instead, I said, "Okay. Cool. We'll let the senior stylists know and they'll reach out to your manager."

He looked at both of us, like he was seeing us clear. "So y'all work here, work here?"

I laughed. "Sort of. We're in a special trainee program."

He looked around the busy room. "That's what's up. Y'all got mad skills. Both of y'all." He put his fist out and we both gave it a knock. "Thanks for the hookup."

"Good luck at the show," Kara said, like it was taking all her energy just to talk.

As soon as he walked out, she started undressing her manny.

We folded clothes silently, side by side. Trying to be nice, I said, "He still liked your outfit. So that's cool."

She didn't look at me as she said, "It's whatever, Mari.

If Magiq like it, then it's dig. It wasn't like I ever stood a chance being teamed against you."

She went into the dressing room to collect clothes, leaving me standing there.

CHAPTER .24.

Mari_Golden:

Am I supposed to feel bad that he liked
my outfit better?

> **Cha-Cha:**
>
> Don't let her ruin it for you. Our
> outfits are gonna be on the RED
> CARPET. Maybe in a pic holding up
> a VGA!! 🎩 🖤 🏆

Mari_Golden:

IKR 😩 How bad are they dragging me
in the chat?

> **Cha-Cha:**
>
> lol you cute. Our chat been 💀

since Saturday. I think they got a
chat w/her friend. Myra? Tyra?

Mari_Golden:

lol Myra.

Cha-Cha:

Yep. I hated being in the middle
anyway.

Mari_Golden:

Why cause you didn't want lose your
job? lol

Cha-Cha:

I mean, yes. Ha ha. Also, you good
peoples.

Mari_Golden:

Why everybody acting like I was going
to run back and tell on them like we in
second grade? 😒

Cha-Cha:

No lies, I thought that the first
few days. But Justice said you was
chill. I rolled w/that. And you are
chill. Don't worry about how Kara
feels.

Mari_Golden:

I haven't done anything to her. Why
doesn't she like me?

Cha-Cha:

That was it. Sometimes you have to shrug it off.

After Marques and Joel announced, officially, that
Chandra and I had won the challenge, they sprung on us
that we were all going to get to attend the VGAs.

I really thought everything was going to be cool after
that. We were going to the hottest awards show of the
summer. Like Joel said, we were experiencing something
together that no other people in the world were going
through.

In the world.

That kind of got me. I didn't want to be irked every
time I thought about this summer. Boo on that energy.

I didn't ignore Justice and Kara. I didn't not ignore
them either.

We had a way of making the cavernous storeroom feel
small. It was how everybody always ended up around the
steam racks. Partly to keep the person steaming company,
and partly to gloat a little over not drawing the short straw
and having to steam. I'd backed down from claiming the

runner job and was the steam sucker this time.

All the running and planning of VGAs felt like a dream. All that was left was packing up the outfits and getting them to the clients. That wasn't our job. Huffing steam at wrinkled clothes was our job. Tagging shoes and putting cart full after cart full of clothes, back onto the racks, was our job.

Nobody pretended anymore that we were a group of four.

It was Justice and Kara. It was me and Chandra.

If we weren't in pairs, we had music whispering into our ears from our phones, blocking out the silence between us.

Chandra was supposed to be clear across the room logging in shoes and making sure they were in the right cubby, but she sat at a table a few feet from me with a big pile in front of her, tagging and logging the shoes on the sheet. Every few minutes she'd disappear with a pile and come back with a new pile.

Kara was working with me. She kept herself busy on her phone, waiting, until I hung a few freshly steamed pieces on the rack.

Whenever Justice got back from rounding up clothes, he'd text her. I only knew that because she'd yell her answer across the room as he was on his way back out.

Me and Chandra exchanged a "I know" eyeroll, every time.

"Do you already know what you wearing to the show?" Chandra asked, loud, so I'd hear her over my music.

I tugged the bud from my right ear.

"Not really."

She wiped down a pair of tennas. "Do you think they would ever let us check out something from the inventory?" She looked around at the bounty.

Kara snorted. "If Mari ask, I bet they will."

Chandra looked hopeful.

I ignored the comment and gestured to the dress I'd just finished steaming. "You can take this one." I ran the hand steamer down its arm one last time. Much as I hated steaming, I took satisfaction in watching a wrinkled mass of fabric come out crisp and pretty. The steam billowed in my face for a few seconds before poofing away to the high ceiling.

"Are you talking to me?" Kara asked. She stared at the dress, mouth pooched, like it was going to climb into her hands on its own, before throwing darts at me with her eyes.

"Yeah," I said, biting back the sarcasm itching its way up my throat.

"Well, then, call my name if you talking to me." She folded her arms and mugged at me. "Don't just be talking at me."

"Why do you have to take everything so personally?" I asked.

I heard Chandra mutter, "Aww man, here we go," under her breath.

I put the steamer on its hook, calmly, like confronting people was my thing. It was the opposite of my thing. My muscles were coiled tight, ready to hit or run until I saw that Kara's face was lit up. I had set something off. She seemed happy about it.

I searched in my mind over the few words I'd just spoken, wondering what I'd said to give her that "aww yeah" smirk.

It was going down and she wanted it to.

My stomach churned as I stood my ground.

She crossed her arms. "I guess I do take things personally. Especially with people running round telling other people that I'm playing them." The news had the effect she wanted. Her eyes had a nasty glint to them. "Yeah, Justice told me what you said."

Of course he had. Ol' fake gopher-acting, I-can-do-more-than-play-basketball-but-my-feelings-hurt-when-somebody-say-something-bad-about-my-outfit self.

My adrenaline pumped. I felt the pulse in my palm as I gripped the steamer. I talked through my tongue, thick and dry. "It's not like you care what I think about you."

"I don't." She waved it off. "You just mad because me and him get along and got more in common than you have with him." Her hands went to her hips. "Y'all probably only friends 'cause he wanted to get into the program."

I shook my head, refusing to fall into her trap. "Yeah, all right. Look, the dress is ready for you to rack."

I turned my back and was about to reach for another blouse when she rolled up on me and pushed my shoulder.

"If you knew what was good, you wouldn't be turning your back on me, Marigold," she warned.

Chandra was up in an instant. "Don't do that, Kara," she said in a low calm voice. "It don't have to be like that."

Her head swiveled, looking around for any adults. But with VGA selections over, the storeroom was all ours again. Kara brushed Chandra's arm off her shoulder and glared at me.

"Let's just stay out of each other's way," I said, managing to keep the tremor out of my voice but not my hands. I played it off by placing my hand on top of the rack full of dresses and blouses next to me. It steadied my nerves just enough for me to go on. "You been wanting smoke with me from day one." I straightened up, determined not to be cowed. "I'm above it."

"Of course, you think you are," she spat. "You don't know me, Marigold. You really don't know me."

"How can I not? You announce it every time you open your mouth," I said. I imitated her in an annoying high-pitched whine. "We not gonna be friends. I don't need nobody to help me, I got this. I'm not scared of no Marques." More Kara-isms formed in my head, but I shut it down. "We all know who you are. You never let us forget."

She was speechless, so I took the time to set one more thing straight.

"And for real, I don't care what's going down between you and Justice."

"Ay, whoa," Justice said as he came in on us. He stood across from me, like the four of us were set for a game of foursquare. He looked from Kara to me. "What's going down between Justice and who?"

"You still think this is about Justice?" Kara said, smirk so deep, it dimpled her chin.

Chandra looked on, confused and curious.

"What is about me?" Justice demanded, but he looked anxious.

"Nothing is about you," Kara said. She looked me up and down, long and hard. "Hmmph, we even have the same eyes. But we ain't the same in no other way, that's for sure."

I frowned. "What are you talking about?"

Her expression lost its hard edge for a few seconds. She cut her eyes at me, untrusting.

"You really don't know, do you?" she asked, in the same gentle voice I'd only ever heard her use with Magiq. I barely had time to digest the quiet shock in her voice before she turned her lips up in disapproval and the regular Kara was back. "All this yours." She gestured to the huge room and everything in it. "But you ain't the only princess of the Flexx Unlimited empire." Her voice was mean, taunting, as she said, "They say you can take the dog out the streets but you can't take the streets out the dog."

We were all rooted in our spots. Justice's face was pained. He rubbed at his eyebrow, the other hand behind his head. He was leaning back a little like he didn't want to catch the words Kara was throwing at me.

Seeing I still didn't understand, she sucked her teeth loud and threw her hands in the air.

"We sisters, Marigold." She sat on the edge of the table piled high with shoes and crossed her feet daintily like she'd just announced today was Monday. "I'm your father's little secret. The skeleton in his closet."

"What?" I whispered thickly. I slowly backed up against the rack of steamed clothes. The steamer hissed softly in my hand. I shook my head, trying to shake out the bells ringing in my ears.

Sisters.

Me and her?

"Mari, you okay?" Chandra asked, looking from me to Kara like she was looking at ghosts. "Come on, Kara, that's not funny." There wasn't much conviction in it. She looked worried.

I felt sick to my stomach with them all staring at me like I'd just landed from a spaceship.

I caught a look between Kara and Justice. A squint, like he disapproved, a shrug from her.

I turned on him, eyes blazing. "She already told you?"

"I—she," he stuttered.

"And you believe her?" I said, thumping myself against the rack to avoid his reaching hand. The rack rocked before falling over with a loud clatter that made us all jump.

"He believe me 'cause it's true," Kara snapped. She looked back at me, curiously, then said matter-of-fact, in case I missed it, "What I gotta lie for? Marshall Johnson is my father."

"That's how you got into Style High?" I asked dumbly.

"Yep, Daddy pulled some strings, I guess," she said, with a high-pitched laugh that hurt my ears.

I winced at the word *Daddy*. I wanted to sit down, but the nearest chair was five steps away. I wouldn't make it.

She glared. "Yeah, guess it's gonna take a minute for you to get used to somebody else being able to say that, huh?"

I swallowed hard, forcing spit down my dry throat. I sat perched on the edge of the shoe table just in case my legs decided not to work.

"Why would I believe you, Kara?" My breathing was hard, trying to keep the words shooting out of my mouth, unable to stop them once they started. "Any hood rat who even barely knew my father back in the day could probably claim they hooked up with him. And my parents are always helping somebody from around the way to get a start in life. You're just another one of their charity cases." Her eyes bucked and I forced the rest out before I lost my nerve. "From the start you came in hating me."

"I came in hating you?" she accused. "Please. You were up on your throne, day one. Acting like I had to explain why I was here." She looked around at the others and her voice broke. "Acting like I was just some leftover trash that got forced on you. Thinking your skills so much better than everybody else's. Thinking you better, period."

It didn't sway me.

"So, you're the one left out?" I asked. "You haven't done nothing but clown me. Or try to intimidate me and . . ." I almost said, Turn Justice against me. I squeezed the words back down my throat. Not even with this whole sister joke was I going to let her shake me. My chest heaved so hard, I had to gulp to get the words out. "You the one that brought smoke, Kara. But go ahead and look dumb running around spreading rumors."

She was up on me in three steps. The curls of her weave jiggled, coily angry worms, as she went off.

"You don't need to believe me. That's what little Hill girls do anyway, hide from what's right in front of 'em." She thrust her finger in my face. "I'mma give you a pass on calling my momma a hood rat. This time. And I'm only giving you that pass because you too stupid to recognize the truth when somebody tell it to you." She was shaking and the fire in her voice matched mine, but she managed to keep it on simmer as she took her turn reading me. "And if I wanted to fight you, it would have been done. Probably everybody in this room know that's word."

"Whatever," I said. "You doing all this over a dude?"

"This not about Justice, Marigold." There was pity and disgust on her face. "Your parents and their little 'deal' made my life hell, so I returned the favor."

The word *deal* stopped me cold. Nobody was better at making deals than my parents.

It felt wrong. So wrong. But the anger in her eyes was real. It hit me, solid in my heart like a block of ice.

She wasn't lying.

I willed myself to stand, unable to stop searching her face. We did both have wide brown eyes. Ms. Sadie called it "doe-eyed." There was even a filter on my camera in case I wanted extra doe-y eyes. But so what? Plenty of people had big eyes.

Us being sisters didn't make sense. Except she'd said, "the deal your parents made." Not the deal your father made. A deal they'd made. I smashed my palms against my temples, trying to shut off the words echoing in my head and couldn't.

Making deals was a Marshall and Manita Johnson specialty.

How many times had I sat there only half listening while they puzzled one together?

But those things were business. This was personal.

How could they have left me out?

They wouldn't have left me out of something like this. Would they?

They had.

Would they?

They had!

The truth smashed into me so hard I took a step back. I lashed out at Kara.

"We sisters, huh? So, I'm supposed to run out crying?" My voice louder with each question. "Run and ask my father if it's true? What?" I shrieked.

Just then Marques and Joel rushed in, Marques in front, his steps crisp and fussy, his waxed eyebrows already in a WTF-esque peak, Joel right behind moving fast for someone his size.

"That's enough," Marques said, stepping directly between me and Kara. It was like being cut from a fishing line. My body sagged as he fussed. "We're upstairs wondering where our runner is and look at the security camera and see you all in here acting a fool."

He looked from me to Kara, mentally pinpointing who to blame before knighting me the winner.

"Come on, Mari." His fingers wiggled at me. "Come with me."

"Why do I have to go with you?" I jabbed at Kara. "She started it."

I sounded two years old and felt it.

"Just come with me . . . please," Marques pleaded softly. Gentle was so odd on him, I gave in. His hand stayed at the small of my back, guiding me past Kara and Chandra. "You good with these three," he asked Joel as we passed.

"Yeah, I have it," Joel said, touching my arm lightly.

I wondered who else had seen and heard us on the cameras.

Marques rubbed at the small of my back, the way you do somebody when you feel sorry for them. As soon as we got into the elevator I burst into tears.

CHAPTER .25.

I sat in the empty waiting area of Daddy's office while he talked to Marques. The silence was so thick, I thought I'd gone deaf until I heard the hum of a far-off vacuum. My thoughts were a super-fast carousel, whipping between Kara's a liar, a total liar. And, My parents lied.

For half a second, I stopped on the Kara's a liar. If she was really my sister, why didn't she demand to come with us to talk to Daddy? Then Marques opened the doors, his eyes sad under his perfectly manicured brows, and the hope that it was all Kara's idea of an ugly joke shattered.

"It'll be all right, Mari," he said, giving my shoulder a confident pat before striding to the elevators.

My mother appeared at the door. She looked somber,

like someone had died. It made me mad. What was she sad for?

"Come on in, baby girl," she said. "We have some explaining to do."

I walked past her open arms and into the huge office. Compared to the screaming voices in my head, the office was serene. A saxophone riff serenaded from speakers well hidden within the one wall that wasn't windows.

My father sat, hunched over, his head in his hands in the area set up with several small sofas and chairs.

He looked up as I walked in. I slouched onto the sofa as far from him as possible.

I forced myself to focus on the sound of the jazz, picking out the plinking of the piano and the sax's gentle cry, while I stared out the windows at the DC cityscape. Usually, the sofa faced east, toward Marks. Now it faced west. I took in the new view. Far beyond a mass of trees that had to be Grovenor's Park was a clump of buildings. Three, maybe four of them. It was hard to tell, because they were hazy from this far away. If it were a cloudy day, they'd be invisible from Flexx. I stared at them, dumbly. They weren't familiar and yet they were. Then it hit me. It was Holly Heights. I was staring right at Kara's neighborhood, maybe even her building. Tears leaked down my face.

My mother was by my side.

"I know we owe you an explanation," she said, talking low directly into my ear.

"We?" I asked, looking up at my father. He stayed silent.

"We were going to tell you," she said. "When the program ended."

I edged away from her so I could see her face. Her lips were pressed together in anger, but her eyes were glossy with unshed tears. Still, the word *we* sank in, letting me know that I was the only one on the outside. My throat closed up. I hung my head and stared at my hands lying limp in my lap. I let my anger boil over into words. "Every morning I had bubble gut trying to tell myself that if I was nicer or quieter or—" I swiped at my tears, looked up, and stared at the buildings on the horizon. "Just be some other way so Kara wouldn't always be so mean to me."

Daddy's head popped up. His face was a mix of concern and anger. "Mean to you how?"

"Why does it matter?" I snapped. "At least now I understand why she hates me."

"Hate is a strong word," Daddy said.

I glared at him and he pressed his lips together, closing off whatever he wanted to say.

My mother scooted closer, closing the gap I'd made between us. She rubbed my arm. "Mari, it's complicated."

"Not really. Kara is my sister. We're the same age . . ." My head swiveled between my parents. "Who's older? Her or me?"

She sighed. "That doesn't matter, Mari."

"It does to me," I exploded. "Who's older?"

"She is," my mother said, throwing my father a look. "Her birthday is in April."

She was four months older than me. It ripped a hole in my heart.

She was the real Flexx princess, not me.

The thought clanged between my ears, making my head throb.

I bent over and sobbed into my lap. My mother rubbed my back, cooing over my head. "This is a lot. Try and understand that it doesn't change anything. We—"

I jerked up. "It changes everything." A hundred thoughts raced from my brain, heading to my mouth. The one that reached my tongue first was "I don't get it. You and Daddy been together since high school. Had y'all broken up?"

My father flinched and I knew immediately that wasn't it.

"Mari, it's complicated," he said. He pushed himself

upright in the delicate princess chair, attempting to get some of his usual confidence back.

I turned to my mother, wanting her to make it make sense. That's what she did. What I needed her to do now. Needed her to say that my father hadn't cheated on her and that this random girl from Holly Heights wasn't related to me.

"How is it complicated?" I demanded.

Her eyes flitted to my father. She refused to let me cut him out of the conversation. "Daddy has to explain."

I stared straight ahead, keeping my eyes away from the window, where the Holly Heights buildings taunted me. When he realized I wasn't going to look his way, he let out a long, sad exhale.

"I've been on my grind since I was fifteen, Marigold—"

"I thought I was going to hear the part of the story that I didn't know. Not the part we rehearse for interviews," I said, half to my mother, half to the office. I folded my arms.

"Everybody gets one chance, Marigold," he said, the familiar firmness back. My heart pattered nervously, making it easy to stare at anything but him. He went on, "You get one chance to get pissed when you find out that your parents aren't perfect and that they mess up, too. I had my chance with my drug addict mother . . . once. Get it?" The question lingered for only a second. "She was a crackhead and still I only got one chance to speak out of turn. Today is that day for you. So, I'm gonna ignore how you talking to me, because I messed up and you're mad. But I'm still your father."

He let the threat hang there, casually.

I felt his eyes boring a hole in the side of my face. I held my breath until he continued.

"If it hadn't been for Ms. Sadie, I would be dead or in jail by now because my grind could have led to hustling drugs. It didn't." I closed my eyes as his words formed pictures in my head of him and his brothers. Them going off to jail one by one, returning home and then each getting gobbled up by the streets. Uncle Ronnie by gunfire in a robbery. Uncle Brian by overdose, just like my real grandmother. And then Uncle Kevin shot down by a rival dealer. Three uncles that I never knew. I couldn't rightfully shed tears for them; they were only names attached to stories I'd heard so many times. But my head spun, thinking of what my life could have been like if my father's grind had been different. He pushed on unapologetically. "Working is all I know. Me and your mom got that in common."

The smile in his voice infused my heart with the tiniest promise that this would be okay. I couldn't see how. But I wanted it to be. I tried to hope as Daddy went on.

"We were only nineteen." His right thumb was pressing and massaging his palm like it was helping to work the words out of his mouth. "Your mother was a sophomore at Hughes College and I was a hardhead finally getting a break. Word about Flexx was spreading. I was finally making money at it. Real money. And Flexx was about to blow up. Every day I got closer and closer. I could feel it in my bones."

I closed my eyes so I wouldn't scream, I know all this, because this was still the stuff straight out of one of the magazines that told every detail of our lives—the fake side of our lives. Knowing that Kara knew the real side made me feel sick.

I guess my face, even with my eyes closed, must have shown my impatience because he sped up.

"We were teenagers with big dreams. I had a legitimate hustle that had to work and I was helping however I could to make sure your mom got her degree. Seemed like I was trying to hold the world up on my shoulders. So, I went out and did something stupid. Maybe needing to feel like every move I made wasn't a life-or-death situation." He took a deep breath and confessed. "I went to a party, met Kara's mother, and started a short side relationship with her."

I cringed, squeezing my eyes tighter shut against the words *side relationship* and jumping when I felt Daddy come sit next to me. His voice bassed softly. "I ended it with her as soon as I found out Mommy was pregnant with you. I didn't know Carla was pregnant until Kara was a year old. At the time I thought my infidelity was the stupidest thing I'd ever done. But I realize the stupidest thing was how we . . . how I handled it."

My eyes fluttered open, mostly against my will, but also because now they had me sandwiched as they forced the truth into my brain.

"Daddy has always taken care of Kara," my mother said. "He pays child support and once Flexx was established, he made sure she got even more." Her voice tightened. "But it wasn't enough for her mother."

"I'm not going to make it worse by blaming anybody," my father said quickly. "Me and Carla had an agreement in place."

"A deal," I said dryly.

"Yeah, I guess you could call it that," he said, apparently missing the venom in my voice. "We agreed we'd go our separate ways as long as I paid her monthly and set up a trust for Kara. I thought she was still in North Carolina with relatives. I didn't know she'd moved back here last year. I hadn't heard anything from her for years until a few months ago." He touched my arm. "And I know you don't really care about all that. You're pissed because you have a sister and you didn't find out from us . . . from me." The chair creaked as he sat back. His voice choked up. "You didn't hear it from me. I violated your trust, the number-one most important thing between a daddy and his daughter."

I glanced at him from the corner of my eye.

"I wasn't the man that I should have been . . . the man that I want some man to be for you one day. I'm sorry, Marigold." He put his head in his hands and wept. "I'm really sorry."

I wanted to throw myself into his lap and cry with him, but my body wouldn't obey my heart. I sat, bowed over like a question mark, staring at the rug, listening to his choked sobs.

"We already have our attorney working on this," my mother said, professional as you please, like that was what I'd been waiting to hear all this time.

Ooh so it's cool, 'cause you got the attorney working on it.

"For what?" I asked, frowning.

"Because Carla broke the agreement," she said, matter-of-fact. She reached for my hand.

"I don't care about that." I jumped up and away from her touch. "I have a—" My voice shook as the word *sister* tried unsuccessfully to roll off my tongue. I spit it out. "I have a whole sister out here. She hates me. And I don't like her either. I'm sure she been having a good time the last few weeks laughing right in my face at us, the fake first family of DC."

"Mari, nobody cares about —" my mother started to say.

"Who else knows?" I asked, hands on my hips, glaring at her.

She looked to my father, but he still didn't have himself together. He rubbed his temples, hiding his eyes from me.

"Who?" I said, hating that I had to beg.

She sat back, legs crossed. Her Cee Oh Oh face in place as she ticked off their co-conspirators.

"Ms. Sadie. Jack and Kim, Kara's aunt and uncle. Ms. Brenda, Kara's grandmother." She sighed, looking up at me like, Isn't that enough?

My heart was thumping so loud I had to swallow twice to clear it out of my ears. But it was in time to hear her say, "Marigold, DC is a large city but it's small." Her face softened. She patted the seat, inviting me to sit back down. Her jaw clenched when I refused. "I'm not going to lie to you—"

I snorted.

You're not going to lie now.

You're not going to lie anymore.

Right.

Her eyebrows shot up in surprise before she got her cool back in place.

"I'm not going to lie to you," she repeated. "The fact that Daddy had an outside child is probably one of District City's worst-kept secrets. But, I mean it, it doesn't change anything."

"You keep saying that. But it's not true," I said. "I knew something was wrong about her being part of the program. She wasn't into it like Justice and Chandra. I didn't get how she was picked." I threw my hands up. "Now I know why she treated me like I . . ." Her words came back to me. I uttered them softly. "Like I stole something from her."

"You always get along with everybody. I thought you and Kara would hit it off," my father said. He smiled up at me weakly. "I really did. And I thought, Well, when I tell her at least they'll already be friends."

The look on my mother's face told me that was 100% his idea.

"It wasn't the best plan. But we thought Carla was going to keep her end of the deal . . . this time," Mommy said. She stood up and put her hands on my shoulders. "When she asked to include Kara in the program, the stipulation was that we get through the summer and then tell both you girls the truth." Her hands massaged gently. "We didn't know Kara knew."

"Well, she did," I said.

"It feels bad, right now." My mother lifted my chin, forcing my eyes to see the sadness in hers. Forcing me to recognize that the betrayal and anger that burned in me, had burned in her once, too. Maybe still did. "But we'll work it out. As a family now. No more secrets," she said.

Any other time I'd believe her. My mother could fix anything. But not this time.

She couldn't fix this.

CHAT-TER

Raychool:

You have a sister now? Dude that's
so wild.

Mari_Golden:

Under the column of obvious 🫠

Raychool:

don't feel bad. Lots of people
have second families

Mari_Golden:

🫢 whut?!

Raychool:

Lana has an older sister by her
dad's first wife.

Mari_Golden:

not the same Rache. AT ALL

Raychool:

why not?

Mari_Golden:

getting re-married is not having
a whole child by someone else
and pretending they don't exist.
Hello!

Raychool:

True. . .so what's she like?

Mari_Golden:

She cool people. We're having a

sleepover this weekend

Raychool:

😦

Mari_Golden:

No Rachel. She hella sarcastic and

always ready to read somebody. AND

she outed that we're hood twins to

Justice and he dropped me for her.

That's what she's like.

Raychool:

What's a hood twin? He didn't

drop you, Mare. He said you won't

message him back and . . .

I didn't feel like hearing anymore. I clicked out of her

text and over to the thread with Chandra.

Cha-Cha:

Are you coming back tomorrow?

Mari_Golden:

one day of feeling like an idiot was

enough. I'm good, thanks.

Cha-Cha:

it's not your fault you didn't know

Mari_Golden:

and yet, here I am

Cha-Cha:

for real, if you had known do you
think y'all would have been closer?

Mari_Golden:

IDK I can't say yes. Can't say no.

Cha-Cha:

I know I'm being nosy again 🙃
Now that it's out what now?

I stared at the question. I wish I knew.

When Justice's "You good?" text came in, my eyes teared up. I wanted to talk about this with him so bad. I couldn't stay mad at him. Not when I needed somebody who might (maybe, please) understand that I was angry, embarrassed, hurt and . . . curious. Curious what the last few weeks would have looked like if me and Kara had both found out at the same time, together.

Would I have still done Style High? Would she?

Having Justice as a friend was the only thing me and her had in common.

I let his text draw me in.

Mari_Golden:

define good 😕

JayRocks:

it is what it is and what your pops
did ain't your fault so let any other
nonsense slide

Mari_Golden:

like how you knew Kara was my sister
and ain't say boo about it? 😠

JayRocks:

aight that's messed up but what
was I gonna say—Ay yo, your pops
ran mad foul on your moms back
in the day?

Mari_Golden:

😕 Eww

JayRocks:

exactly. On my word, I only found
out the day before she told you.

Mari_Golden:

For real?

JayRocks:

FR

Mari_Golden:

Well, not sure I'm ready roll and act

like it don't hurt to know Kara knew

this whole time and I'm walking around

trying be friends w/her

JayRocks:

No shade but not sure you was

really ever trying be friends w/her

Mari_Golden:

okay, you not wrong. I gave her the

energy she gave me and that's word.

JayRocks:

naw you right. the whole thing

wack AF. . .

JayRocks:

it's wack but it's wack for both of

y'all for real 💀

Mari_Golden:

facts. I guess 😳

JayRocks:

I know its real messed up for you.

But I'm not gonna lie. Its messed

up that she living in Holly while

her pops got all this money. Just

saying ain't nobody winning for
real 🙃

Mari_Golden:

dragged

JayRocks:

Sorry.

Mari_Golden:

Me too

CHAPTER .26.

By the time Wednesday blurred into Thursday, I'd gotten good at pretending the world beyond my room didn't exist. When I did step into any other part of the house I nodded, grunted, and shrugged to communicate.

The carcass of my phone sat in the middle of the bed. I'd stopped charging it. At three that afternoon, the last text—wow u ghost for real, from Chandra—had barely bleeped its way through before the screen blinked to black. With its last breath went my motivation to connect with anybody.

Things at home were as dead as my phone. I wanted to be somewhere else, but didn't have any place to go.

Daddy was sullen because I was avoiding him. Mommy

periodically checked in but always backed off when she realized my replies rarely went beyond two syllables. Ms. Sadie talked enough for all of us, filling our heads with the mission's gossip and reminding us that "this too shall pass."

Glad she thought so.

I sketched a few designs, but half-heartedly.

I'd been around styling and fashion all my life. I was naturally drawn to breaking down what made a look work. Now that tug, to hook up a good outfit or create a brand new one, was pieces of my parents I wanted to shed.

Justice was right. None of this was Kara's fault; it was my parents' fault. They were frauds. Then I was too.

All that talk about giving back and never turning away from a chance to make DC's hoods better felt hollow. I was surprised no one had ever laughed dead in their faces or mine and called it what it was—phony.

Kara did. In her own way, at least.

The thought sent a flood of hot shame through me.

All this time, they had been out here cutting checks to community centers while Kara lived in the city's most run-down nabe. My mother kept talking about nothing had changed. She'd even mentioned bringing a lawyer into it because Kara's mom broke their deal.

It was like my parents still thought a contract could make things right.

A contract wouldn't change that Kara was related to me. We were still blood.

There were now two princesses to the Flexx empire. Two. Not one.

And she'd still always be older, making me Princess B.

Every time I admitted it, my head ached.

A part of me missed the rumors of Daddy being a drug dealer. At least they weren't true. I guess.

I wallowed in my misery. I didn't know who I was now that Kara was more than some annoying girl who wore too much lip gloss.

It wasn't hard keeping to myself. My parents still had a business to run and I made sure I was in my room whenever I heard one of them come home. I spent afternoons in the family room, surfing channels; evenings in my room, sitting in the window seat, staring out across the thick trees. Blocks and blocks away was Holly.

Friday, the silence was so loud that I plugged back in.

I lay across the sofa in our family room with the TV blaring, living between my two worlds, hoping one of them would make me feel better.

Raychool:

I'm glad you and Justice made up.

Mari_Golden:

Not sure we did exactly

Raychool:

are u still mad at him? Why?

Mari_Golden:

not mad but things aren't like before
either

Raychool:

even if he knew, not like it would
have been easy for him to tell you.
Don't be too hard on him.

Mari_Golden:

He admitted he knew. Can we drop it,
please?

Raychool:

I don't want it to be weird when
school starts is all.

Mari_Golden:

it can get weirder than I left school an
only child and coming back w/an older
sister? 😒

Raychool:

😀 😀 😀 nope, you totally won that one

Raychool:

j/k but not like you ever have to see her or anything. I bet your mom already has like—cannot come within 20 feet of my real daughter—in the new contract. 😂

I winced at the text. I didn't like Kara but that felt harsh. It was some certified Flowered Arms Academy thinking. So, I said nothing and switched to Chandra's thread.

Cha-Cha:

A 2nd year!! Style High a permanent summer thing. Are you going to come back? You gotta come back, Mari!

Mari_Golden:

Congratulations! *means it*

Cha-Cha:

Thank you!! 😊 fyi Kara stopped coming too. just been me and Justice. 😞

Mari_Golden:

Not really surprised. She probably only
did Style High so she could read me one
good time. 🪦

                                    Cha-Cha:

                        or maybe she just wanted to see
                            her father in real life. 😏

Mari_Golden:

she coulda came for the first day and
then went ghost to do all that

                                    Cha-Cha:

                        True. Will you at least still come
                            to the VGAs Saturday? 🙏

Mari_Golden:

😋 🎧 doubtful

                                    Cha-Cha:

                        I know this easy for me to say
                        but 😤 now that the truth is out,
                        maybe you and Kara should try
                        and talk. Maybe she not that bad.

I sat up, wrapped a blanket around me and scrolled
away from the messages. I looked for something to binge.

After giving up on anything involving music,
fashion, or hip-hop, I found a cooking competition.

Three people ran around a kitchen grabbing at pots and throwing food into pans. The scenes flashed by without me totally seeing them. I thought about Chandra and Rachel's messages.

I loved Rachel, but things at Flo-A moved at a different speed. After the initial juiciness of my scandal, my new sibling wouldn't matter. If Jenna Ripley could survive her mother being caught slipping out of Anthony Luke's father's room on the school trip to New York City, probably I'd survive people knowing I had a half sister. They wouldn't ever meet her, so I could even say it was only a rumor—if I wanted. But no contract would ever determine how this was going to go down in the District City that I lived in with my parents.

Like Chandra said—now that it was out . . .

This was just the beginning.

I shuddered as my phone beeped and tooted.

Chandra had decided to fill my silence with a sermon:

> **Cha-Cha:**
> I know it seems like the world knows your business. . .okay and they sort of do. Hahahas.
> **Cha-Cha:**
> But for really for really even by

now its probz old news and the

streets on to the next.

Cha-Cha:

Don't let it stop u from coming

back next year. Please!!

Cha-Cha:

Style High not the same w/o u. 😉

I hit her back with a message that I hoped would let the issue rest for a little bit:

Next summer a million miles away.

How bout I let u know when it's just a

hundred miles away? 😜

I pushed the phone under a pillow and sank myself into the blanket up to my nose.

My arms were wrapped in the blanket and I was too lazy to take them out to turn the channel, so I let the food show hold me hostage. It was turned up so loud, I didn't hear Ms. Sadie until she was right over me. I jumped when she called my name.

"Marigold, turn that TV down, girl. I been calling you the last five minutes." She picked up the remote and stabbed it at the TV until the volume was on whisper. "Justice is here."

"I don't want . . . ," I said until I saw Justice standing at the door of the family room.

"If you had answered me five minutes ago, you could have told me that and I would have saved the boy some embarrassment," Ms. Sadie said, head shaking as she exited.

My heart beat double time. I wasn't sure if it was because I was afraid he'd heard me say I didn't want to see him or anxiety that he was there. It thumped harder as he sat down, leaving a cushion between us.

"Hey," he said, rubbing his hands on his cargo shorts, back and forth, smoothing unseen wrinkles away.

"Hey," I said, but my mouth was still under the blanket so it came out "heh."

I kept my eyes on the TV until he slapped his thighs and took a deep breath.

"I'm sorry that things got all wild."

The silence between us expanded so that even the low buzz of the TV was loud. His Adam's apple bobbed up and down three times in a row, like it was trying to escape.

My fingers gripped the blanket, keeping it mummied around me, letting my words filter through the fabric.

"You know what it feels like?" I focused on the chefs running around on screen. "Like I'm a video game everybody thinks they can start over when they mess up a level." I shook the blanket off and picked up the remote. I ran my fingers over the raised buttons to have something to do with my hands. "You acted brand-new from the start, like you didn't want people to know we were close." I finally looked at him as I said, "Unless I been wrong and we weren't ever close."

"It's not like that, Marigold." His Adam's apple bobbed like crazy. I forced my eyes to stay on his face. His eyebrows worked up and down, finally freezing in a scowl. He cleared his throat once, then twice. "Kara wasn't the same way with me like she was with you."

I huffed. "Shocker."

"Is it gonna be like this?" he asked, smoothing at the invisible wrinkles in his shorts again. "You gonna keep snapping on everything I say?"

My only answer was lowering my eyebrow. He kept on.

"From the start, Kara was cool peoples." He put both hands up in surrender. "Me and her had a lot in common. She never knew her father, was raised by her moms, was living in a neighborhood where the nonsense always popping off." He shrugged. "Me liking her didn't mean me and you weren't still tight."

I pulled my knees to my chest to hold in the happiness that he still felt there was a me and him.

"At school I can kind of forget who your pops is. Every day at Style High I couldn't." He tugged at the bottom of his shorts, let go, and looked me dead in the eyes. "Kara got in my head. She kept asking if I thought I only got in because we was friends. And—" He shrugged. "I couldn't say for real that wasn't true. It messed me up and I didn't want her or nobody thinking I was gaming you to be there."

"You never care what people think any other time. Why now?" I asked.

He rolled his eyes. "You mean I gotta act like I don't care." The old Justice broke through. "I told you I was tired of always worrying if I was saying or doing the right thing at school. I ain't think I was gonna have to spend my summer doing that." His eyes skittered away from the hurt on my face even as he admitted, "Everybody else had to work to get into Style High. You decide at the last minute you'n got nothing else better to do. And bam you in." He hurried on. "With you there, seemed like I had to watch how I said stuff again."

Hurt sat in my chest like ice cubes. "What did I do to make you feel like that? Seriously?" I asked.

He sucked his teeth in disgust. "Don't act like you wasn't judging her. You was, Mari. Even day one, you was.

Just like everybody else at school do when somebody Black walk in. It reminded me that me and you always gonna see stuff different."

"Okay, see, wait . . ." I pushed the blanket to the floor and sat cross-legged, facing him full-on. "Stop saying I'm just like everybody at school like they be treating me special." I shook my head, refusing to let him interrupt. "They don't, Justice. They don't. The one thing I got in common with them is my parents can afford to send me there. But the first thing they see is I'm Black and that's how they treat me. Only difference is, I don't feel like fighting every time somebody say something sideways, like you do." His head hung as I kept on. "You keep talking about how people at school treat you but then you and Kara did the same thing to me." I choked up. "And it was messed up 'cause I couldn't say anything to anybody because I didn't want nobody thinking I was running and telling my parents things that happened between us."

"I wasn't treating you that way on purpose," Justice said.

"Well, it felt that way. And I was hard on her 'cause she was hard on me," I spat.

"Naw, I know," he said quietly.

For once, he looked remorseful.

"It's messed up when your best friend don't think you Black enough."

"I don't feel like that," he said, hands smoothing his shorts again.

"That's how it comes off, though." I leaned over and touched his thigh. "I get that you feel out of place at Flo-A. I do too, sometimes. If you don't get that then no one will." I sat back again. "I thought we could be ourselves at Style High this summer. I'm sorry it was awkward."

"That was on me. I got in my feelings." He swallowed, looking just past me as he said, "And look, I know I was tripping a lil' bit over the VGA stuff, but only 'cause it felt like you was trying prove something."

"A little bit?" I asked, head cocked.

He smiled. "A lot."

"I wasn't trying to prove anything," I said, folding my arms. "You took it so personal, I didn't know what I could or couldn't say anymore."

He nodded. "I shoulda told you that Kara was talking smack. But I didn't want be the one bringing drama. I swear I didn't know what all the static was from, at first. I woulda never told her what you said about her playing me if I had known—you know, if I knew she was your . . ."

"Sister," I said flatly. "Might as well get used to saying it."

"I wasn't ever trying to dog you." He tugged at the blanket playfully, flashing his famous smile. "I thought if you and Chandra was close, then I could keep things good by being cool with Kara. Then things got mad weird." He shook his head. "Once Kara told me about being your fam, I didn't know how to tell you. Or if I should. For real, I thought she was tripping." His sigh exploded to the ceiling. "I had hoped she was."

"But she wasn't," I said, shoulders sagging as I exhaled. We sat in silence while the TV murmured.

He stood up. "Are we good?"

I nodded. His eyebrow flicked up in question, so I reassured him. "We're good. Congratulations, by the way. Chandra told me y'all got invited back next summer."

"I don't know if I should, though." He grabbed behind his neck, looking nervously toward the doorway of the family room like he expected to see Daddy there. "Your pops might think I was the one that got you and Kara beefing."

I waved it off. "Nope, he know that's all on him." I stood and folded the blanket to have something to do. "Next year you won't be stuck between two sisters."

"Wait, I kind of like how that sounds," he said with a smile.

I threw the blanket at him. "Ew. Don't even."

He laughed. "I'm kidding. You already talking like you not down with it for next year."

I shrugged. "I'm not down for talking about it for sure." We refolded the blanket together. Then I worked up the courage to ask, "When was the last time you talked to Kara?"

"The day after," he said, as if the day Kara announced her place on my family tree was a day of its own like Sunday or Monday. "I asked her was she coming back? And she wrote back, hard pass. I think she blocked me after that."

"You have her address?" I asked.

He glanced at me, confused, as he nodded.

"Text it to me, please."

He pulled up her contact, stared at it. "You sure?"

"No. But give it to me anyway."

CHAPTER .27.

Ms. Sadie's voice hollered from the bottom of the stairs. "Marigold. Nut? Pea Head?"

I scrambled out of my room and raced to the huge landing that looked over the bottom level, heart thudding, thinking maybe she was hurt. She stood at the foot of the stairs, hands on her hips, looking up where she knew faces would appear. My mother came out of their bedroom. I heard my father's heavy footsteps. From where I stood, I could see the top of his head of thick black curls. He stood next to Ms. Sadie.

"All this silence nonsense gone on long enough." Ms. Sadie looked from my father, to me, to my mother with pinched disapproval. "Everybody come on down here into Marshall's den."

She walked into Daddy's office, knowing we'd follow.

There was a slight limp to her step. It was a legitimate limp like something was aching, nothing like her usual little old lady shuffle. She'd aged a few years in the last week, another reminder she wouldn't be there forever. I felt like bursting into tears. Without her I'd be alone.

I pulled up my hood and shrank into it, but not before catching my mother looking at me. There were dark circles under her eyes. I waited until she took a few steps and then came down behind her, slow like a chopping block was waiting for me.

My father sat behind his desk, looking small in his king chair today.

I threw myself dramatically onto the small antique sofa. I snuggled deeper into my hoodie and sank my hands into its pocket. I scooted over as far as I could when my mother sat next to me and pretended not to see the hurt in her eyes.

Ms. Sadie stood in the middle of the room, glaring. None of us were exempt from her scorn.

"The last week been the hardest of my life." As soon as she started talking, her voice broke.

She hobbled over to the desk and leaned against it. "I was giving y'all three time to work this out. But everybody too caught up in how they feel to think about anybody else." She looked directly at me. "Family is family no matter how bad they mess up. You think this the first time your momma and daddy done something that ain't make no sense?"

I wasn't sure how to answer that. It didn't matter. She went on, not waiting for one.

"And it ain't gonna be the last." She pushed off the desk and thrust a knotted finger at my father. "But you was wrong for trying to hide your mistakes, Pea Head. If you was gonna go through all the trouble of bringing them two girls together, you oughta sat them down and talked to them from the start. Prepare them for the nonsense people out on the street gonna be saying about them, so they got each other in it."

He hung his head for a second, then manned up and looked Ms. Sadie in the eye, nodding his assent.

"Mari, I'm human," my father said solemnly. "I didn't handle the situation well. I want you to understand that what I did, I did because I thought it was the best way. Your mother wanted to tell you, up front. But I thought if you and Kara spent a few weeks working together, maybe it would take a little of the edge off the shock." His chair squeaked as he got up. I kept my eyes down. His kicks, clean like they'd just come out the box, came into view. His deep voice floated above my head. "You're my baby girl. If you think . . ." There was an odd clucking in his throat. He pushed through it. "That this means I love you less or that you have to step aside to make room for Kara, it would break my heart."

He came closer. I looked up. When I did, he took my cheeks into his big hands and planted a kiss on my forehead.

I reached for his shoulders. His arms went around my waist. He held on as long as I held on. My mother leaned in and joined the hug, cocooning me between them.

I hoped if I stayed there long enough, everything else would just melt away. I wanted it to work that way, so bad.

"It'll be okay," my mother whispered. "Honesty from this point forward. We promise."

She kissed my ear and rubbed my back.

Finally, I let go. My father pecked me on the nose.

"I love you, Marigold." The gold flecks that danced in his brown eyes when he was excited had taken the night off. In their place was a red dullness. "I'm going to do right by you. Never think this changes that you're my heart."

I wanted to believe him, but my heart ached, knowing I wasn't his only girl anymore. And nothing he said could change that.

"Sure this ain't news to you, but your daddy ain't the first man to have an outside child," Ms. Sadie scoffed. "Now that you know, it's time to move on. That child is your sister, whether you like it or not, Mari Henny."

Ms. Sadie went on like I'd challenged her.

"You may not want a sister. But that wasn't your decision to make. Point is you have one." Her voice lowered but was no less biting. "And the way you feeling, right now, betrayed with your trust crushed, that's how that little girl felt. And for longer than you. And that's why she started all that trouble."

"I'm supposed to feel sorry for her?" I snapped. It was bad enough I had to share Daddy, I didn't like Ms. Sadie feeling all sorry for Kara, too. She surprised me, ignoring my disrespect.

"I can't tell you how to feel about her, Marigold," she said softly. She scooted her small body between me and my mother and took my hands in hers. Her hands were rough and hard, but her touch was what I needed. I let the tears fall. "None of us got the right to tell you not to be sad or mad. Or tell you how long you should feel that way." She lowered her head and looked up into the recesses of my hoodie. Her eyes were bright with unshed tears. "But you ain't the only one whose world been turned upside down."

I wanted to snatch my hands away and put them over my ears, but she had a grip like she knew what I was thinking.

"I'm not going to feel sorry for her, Ms. Sadie," I said.

"I already told you, I'm not trying to tell you how to feel," she said, pulling me toward her until I had to look at her. "But the only thing worse than being lied to is living a lie." Her eyes begged as she asked, "Understand?"

I shrugged, even though I did. Sometimes going along with the traditions and rules at school felt like a lie. Even my parents didn't agree with some of the rules at school, but they went along and made sure I did too. At least until we could change them. But it's hard. And sometimes you forget who you are a little bit, when you go along for too long. Justice was my loud reminder. The one who gave me a break from it all. I guess he had been Kara's too.

I don't know how long Kara had known Daddy was her father. But I couldn't imagine coming from where she lived every day, knowing what she knew but having to act like it wasn't true. That would have me twisted.

I reluctantly confessed. "Yes, I understand."

"I hope you do. 'Cause your parents lied to you. But that little girl . . . Kara, she was the one living the lie. Knowing who her father was but not being able to do nothing about it 'cause of some agreement her momma made." She sniffed, to make sure we knew how she felt about that. "And it made her angry and sad and like she wanted to hurt somebody. That how you feel?"

I shrugged again. I expected Ms. Sadie to dig in and fight me, make me admit I knew exactly what she meant. Instead, she patted my hand. Disappointment radiated from her.

"All right. All right. Stubborn like your momma. Well, this the last thing I'm gonna say—what you feel for that girl is in your heart. So that's your own business. Even if me and your momma and daddy expect you to feel a certain way, if you don't truly feel it, it don't amount to nothing. But now it's all out there. The smoke cleared and truth is, you still got two parents trying help you through this who can get you what you want and what you need. Even with the truth out there, what Kara have?"

She squeezed my hand then and limped out of the room, leaving me feeling like dirt.

CHAPTER .28.

The next morning, I beat the sun up, debating with myself.

For fourteen years I'd had a sister. A sister. Somebody I could have complained to. Cried with. Laughed with. Somebody who would get it when I rolled my eyes at Daddy's corny jokes or when he'd start going off about our generation gutting hip-hop for its crops and leaving the fields dusty and barren.

For fourteen years, my parents had lied to me about her. Even Ms. Sadie had lied. And Kara's mother had lied too.

I told myself to stay mad at Kara, the way she'd treated me all summer, how she turned Justice against me—but nothing would stick. We'd both been lied to. The difference was, I had everything and she didn't have anything.

That pushed me out of the bed.

I thought about every argument me and Kara had over the summer. I'd been fighting over who knew more, whose side Justice would take; and Kara had been fighting for her right to be who she really was, a Johnson. It still sucker punched me in the stomach, but she had as much right to Daddy's name as I did. I didn't want to share it, but that wasn't my choice. It hadn't been for a long time.

I took the Metro to her house and watched the landscape go from bustling to abandoned.

Years of visiting Marks Park didn't prepare me for the swing set with no swings, a large area that had to have been grassy at one time but was now just dirt with strangled patches of brittle brown weeds. The building that went on forever—brick after ugly brown brick; a high-rise made up of windows without screens.

A few little kids were outside already, hanging around the basketball court, chasing one another in a game of tag.

I passed by a skinny dude standing at the building's entrance and steeled myself for a catcall. He didn't disappoint.

"You come for me, Ma?" He grinned, leering at me. "I got something for you."

I kept my pace even and my face neutral. I had no doubt the dude would follow me if I let on how scared I was.

It smelled like pee inside the hallway. The stench was everywhere, like it had been smeared on the walls and sprayed on the floors. I walked up the dirty, dank stairs without touching anything, praying no one would come down, forcing me to inch closer to the wall or rail.

Thankfully, Kara lived on the third floor. Still, I was winded by the time I got to the landing. I took a few breaths before knocking.

"Who the hell is that this early?" a voice demanded from behind the door.

I forced strength into my voice. "Marigold . . . Johnson."

I expected every door on the floor to open so people could gawk. But it stayed quiet in the thick, muggy hallway. Light from the caged window at the end didn't reach as far as Kara's door. I inched closer, afraid of what might pop out of the dimness beside me.

The humidity seeped into my skin and sweat popped up everywhere. Moisture spread under my arms and breasts.

Finally, the door opened. It wasn't whoever who had demanded my identity; it was Kara.

Without her rings and fake hair, our resemblance smacked me in the face.

That small nose was my father . . . our father. Her lips were full and dark, too, like his. Her hair was in two braids that hung to her shoulders. If she'd ever come to work like that, with her own hair and minus all the other accessories, I think anybody would have been right to say, "Hey, y'all look alike."

Standing there finally facing her, I didn't know what to say.

Kara didn't have that issue.

"What, Mari?" Her hip jutted as she waited, blank faced.

I found my voice. "Can we talk?"

She walked away leaving the door open. My only invitation.

The low murmur of a television came from a back room. I tried not to stare, but I couldn't help it. This was where my sister lived.

The apartment was clean. I chastised myself for assuming it wouldn't be. Kara had never looked sloppy. She overdressed but she dressed nice. And she always smelled like Rafella, the same perfume I wore sometimes. But walking up the funky stairway, I'd had a million pictures of what the apartment would look like. Oversized worn furniture that took up so much of the room there wasn't space to walk, a few paintings on the wall, and a shelf full of books wasn't one of them.

There were only two places to sit. Beside her on the fat mint-green sofa or at the table behind it, piled high with mail and magazines.

I sat at the opposite end of the couch, unsure where to start.

She scowled. "I know you didn't come here expecting me to apologize or something."

"I don't know why I came here," I admitted numbly.

The whole ride on the Metro, I'd been angry at my parents and, at first, even Ms. Sadie. But she'd wanted them to tell me the truth. So, I let my anger at her go. But the anger at my parents kept me going even as I entered a part of District City I'd only ever seen rolling through for a charity drive. Now that anger was gone, like it had only been in me to fuel me enough to get here. Tiny goose bumps rose on my arms as the chill of indecision and slight regret sank in. For a minute, I thought maybe I was dreaming. In a few seconds, I'd wake up needing to share my dream of the worst summer of my life with somebody.

But it wasn't a dream. I was in Holly sitting across

from a girl who was built like me, looked a little like me, and yet couldn't be more different than me.

I threw my hands up. "I don't know why I came, Kara. It just seemed like . . . I had to."

Her eyes scanned my face. She must have found the truth in it because she pulled a pillow onto her lap and plucked at it, the nasty scowl nowhere to be found. She sank back into the sofa. She threw her head back and laughed. A sad, defeated sound.

"Seeing you at the door, I was like—yeah, I won. She on my turf." She looked around the apartment, taking inventory of her "turf." "But what I win?"

A fan in the window, behind us, hummed silently as it blew cool kisses at us. It felt good on my hot neck and face.

"I'm so mad," I said finally. My voice was as sad as Kara's laugh. Her eyebrows went up and I answered their question. "Not at you, at my . . . our father. And at my mother." I nodded toward the back of the apartment and lowered my voice. "And at your mother."

"You don't need to whisper." She laughed for real this time. "When she heard it was you, she came running back to my room. 'Kara, Marshall's other daughter at the door. Go handle that.'" Her head shook, but the old tough Kara made an appearance. "Now how she gonna tell me to handle something she started?" She looked over at me, head cocked. "It's pretty messed up."

"For both of us," I said firmly. Then it hit me what she'd said. I repeated it, incredulous. "Marshall's other daughter."

I turned my face so the fan could kiss my burning cheeks.

"Technically, I guess I'm his other daughter, but whatever." She shrugged. "Stuff's been messed up for me for a long time. I'm used to it."

She blinked fast a few times and swiped quickly at the corner of her eyes.

"I still gotta get used to knowing my life is a total lie. Knowing my parents hid an entire person's existence got me way twisted," I said.

To my horror, tears started dripping down my face.

I wiped them away. They kept falling.

Kara scooted down next to me. The fruity essence of Rafella tickled my nose as she leaned in. Her knee touched my thigh, but she stopped short of hugging me.

I sniffed and pulled myself together. I had so many questions.

"When did your mother tell you?" I asked first, needing to know how long she'd lived with the truth.

"New Year's Eve."

She looked resigned and I felt the same way. "She'd heard about the program and it just set her off. She started fussing, saying stuff like, 'Oh, he want help poor kids, do he? But not his daughter . . . yeah, all right, we'll see." She let out a long breath. "For real, she was drinking. I figured she was just tripping. But later she asked me to come look at something. It was your . . ." Her eyes fluttered as she avoided the word, then she pushed out. "Marshall was on TV doing this interview at the ball drop in New York."

Me and Mommy had been just off screen while he was interviewed. I shivered. One more thread connecting us, slowly weaving a web that would entangle us come June.

"She was like, 'That's your daddy.' And I just laughed, like, 'Yeah, all right, Ma,'" Kara said, frowning at the memory. "She was like, 'Oh it's right . . . it's right. And he gon give you a job this summer. This summer you getting what's yours.'" She plucked at the pillow for a few seconds, silent, before going on. "I still didn't believe her. But then in early June she came home one day and said she hoped I was ready to be a Johnson 'cause I started work in a few days."

"You ever ask about it before that?" I asked. "Who your father was, I mean?"

The look on her face made me feel stupid for asking.

"Of course," she said. "But until then she'd always just said, 'Don't worry about it. One day you won't even care.'"

We sat in somber silence, stewing in our own thoughts.

"Mari . . ." She cleared her throat. "I'm sorry for doing it the way I did."

I was grateful for the apology, but it was a little late for that. Not like I could walk out of her apartment and be like, Nice knowing you, and never see her again. Were we really gonna live a twenty-minute Metro ride away and pretend the other didn't exist?

We didn't have any choice but to figure out how to live with the truth.

"It's not your fault," I said, meaning it.

She rose up, surveying my face the way she does, like she's a living lie detector scanning for the truth.

I withstood her scrutiny, never looking away from her.

"I mean, well, it sort of is," she said, nudging me with her knee.

And this time she was crying a little as she laughed.

I knew exactly how she felt, but I was done crying.

Kara's mother eventually came out of the bedroom. She was a slight woman, light skinned, with a shock of red and burgundy braids in a bun nearly as big as her whole head. She came out smoking a cigarette, gritting on me like she wasn't happy that I had come. But what of it?

She had been the one that wanted Kara to get what was rightfully hers.

Well, guess what? She's my daddy's daughter. She's my sister. The title was rightfully hers.

Like it or not.

EPILOGUE

Kara came in hating me.

I was an uppity Hill girl, to her. I was everything she wasn't until she realized where we lived didn't have anything to do with what was in our hearts.

And she was just another of Mommy and Daddy's charity cases to me. Taken on to prove they were still Pea Head and Nut from around the way. Until I learned that everything done for the right reason isn't always right.

We would have met with or without Justice. I know that now.

In a strange way, the three of us were puzzle pieces that clicked together after being turned every which way.

You know they fit, but it takes you a few tries before they snap into place.

Having a sister is . . . different.

Kara and I aren't best friends. Don't go thinking that.

It's more like friends by circumstance. Like when two people's moms are best friends and they're together all the time, so you might as well get along. And who knows how close you'll grow if you're together enough.

Once it was 100% out and confirmed that Marshall Johnson of Flexx Unlimited had a teenage daughter . . . another teenage daughter, things moved fast.

Given a choice, Kara's mother, Miss Carla, might have wished she honored the original contract rather than have Mommy step in and Cee Oh Oh their lives. Then again, maybe not.

Within a month, Kara and her mother had moved into Ms. Sadie's house, rent free. It's cool having the house full again even if Miss Carla does act like I'm the one intruding when I stop over.

Ms. Sadie already loves Kara. Who knew, but Kara likes to cook.

The second I caught myself getting jealous as they clucked and laughed over simmering pots of gravy and greens, Ms. Sadie put her hands on her tiny hips and said, "Ain't nothing stopping you from joining us," and it reminded me that chef-ing really wasn't my thing. I settled for watching, happy when Kara went out of her way to ask me to try whatever she was making and rolling with Ms. Sadie's punches as she constantly dropped that she was glad "somebody" was going to learn her recipes.

And that somebody will also officially become a Flowered Arms Academy Magnolia 112 this fall. She doesn't want to, but me and Justice are tap-dancing around the wack parts and boosting up the good—the Fall Fair, Café Mag, and the track team. She's not totally convinced but I'm kind of looking forward to it. I've been the only Black girl long enough. And even though I doubt the Mags are ready for Kara, our prep school could stand a little sprinkle of Holly spice.

Even without the big earrings, one too many accessories, and long weave, Kara will stand out at school. I'm ready to have her back. Not that she needs anyone to do that. But, if I'm keeping it a stack, that's when people need you to stand by them the most—when they're being exactly who they are.

Now that we know each other better, I hope she'll have mine, too. I'm ready to stop waiting for permission to be who I am. No apologies. No explaining. Time to be happy with the people who rock with me being all of me. As for the people who don't?

They not keeping it real.

★ "Chase writes the diverging, formative experiences of young Black girls beautifully." —*School Library Journal* (starred review)

"A timely middle-grade title." —*Booklist*

"Readers will be keen to see what's next." —*Bulletin of the Center for Children's Books*

"Readers will root for Sheeda and Mo's friendship from beginning to end." —*The Horn Book*

"Fun and juicy." —*New York Times*

"Chase delivers a contemporary narrative on the complexities of race, class privilege, and interpersonal relationships." —*Publishers Weekly*

"A story of summer growth and exploration." —*Kirkus Reviews*

"Will resonate with tweens and teens." —*Booklist*